The Sinister Swaps

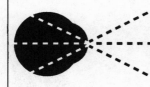

The Sinister Swaps

CHURCH CHOIR MYSTERIES

Hm 284 9

14.95

LT-AF

7/04

Evelyn Minshull

Walker Large Print • Waterville, Maine

ISBN 1-4104-0138-3 (lg. print : sc : alk. paper)

In appreciation of Melanie, middle daughter, and her partner-in-parody husband, Dave. For several months, daily doses of Melanie's mischievous motivation kept me laughing . . . and writing!

As the Founder/CEO of NAVH, the only national health agency solely devoted to those who, although not totally blind, have an eye disease which could lead to serious visual impairment, I am pleased to recognize Thorndike Press★ as one of the leading publishers in the large print field.

Founded in 1954 in San Francisco to prepare large print textbooks for partially seeing children, NAVH became the pioneer and standard setting agency in the preparation of large type.

Today, those publishers who meet our standards carry the prestigious "Seal of Approval" indicating high quality large print. We are delighted that Thorndike Press is one of the publishers whose titles meet these standards. We are also pleased to recognize the significant contribution Thorndike Press is making in this important and growing field.

Lorraine H. Marchi, L.H.D.
Founder/CEO
NAVH

★ Thorndike Press encompasses the following imprints: Thorndike, Wheeler, Walker and Large Pr int Press.

1

Gracie Lynn Parks deeply inhaled the scent of roses. The grounds of Pleasant Haven Retirement Community were riotous with them: from ramblers the color of vine-ripened tomatoes to tea varieties in shades from peach through paprika to that unique purple-black of eggplant. One rampant, spiny bush bore pulpy white blossoms; its newer foliage imitated the lemon-lime hue of jalapeño peppers.

In the midst of such floral assault, Gracie supposed, most people might not be preoccupied with cooking ingredients, but since she had three upcoming catering assignments crowding her calendar, she found she could think of little else.

"Gather 'round, folks!" Barb Jennings commanded in her bossiest choir director voice. "Gracie, get your mind out of the kitchen and think alto!"

Gracie laughed with the others. They knew her far too well, her dear fellow members of Eternal Hope Community Church!

Uncle Miltie, who had lived with Gracie in Willow Bend since the death of his deeply loved wife three years earlier, pushed his aluminum walker close enough to whisper, "We could set the buffet table near that trellis." Though not a choir member, he'd come along with Gracie for the sake of an outing.

Exactly what she'd been thinking! "A fine idea," she whispered in return. Family Day at Pleasant Haven, the second of her three commitments, was scheduled for a week from Saturday.

"Vocalize!" Using a ballpoint pen in lieu of a baton, Barb led them through the ascending and descending scales.

Lord, thank You, Gracie prayed, even as she carried the alto through the familiar exercises. *Thank You for these friends . . . for the gifts of music and those who produce or even simply appreciate it . . . for the opportunity to aid Pastor Paul in his ministry here . . . for the wonder of roses —*

"Ten minutes," Barb announced. "Not a minute longer. Then we're scheduled to give our concert for the residents."

"Gracie!"

Without turning, Gracie warmed to Amy Cantrell's lilting young voice.

"There's the most beautiful plant beyond the arbor!"

"Of course," Gracie answered, though the question hadn't been asked. "If I recognize it."

"You will," Amy said with supreme confidence. "You always do."

They strolled in companionable silence, their walking shoes thumping slightly on curving walks of multicolored stones. An indefinable fragrance — honeysuckle perhaps — rode a gentle breeze, and a bevy of birds gossiped within heavy screenings of maple and oak.

"I wonder if they're talking about *us* —" Amy began, laughing, then broke off.

Breath suspended, they stood elbow-close, listening.

"A dream is a wish your heart makes," floated a pure voice, as fluid as a spring freshet, as silver as crystal windchimes.

Amy caught Gracie's arm. Gracie hadn't the heart to tell her that her fingernails were carving grooves, perhaps even drawing blood. And she could understand the teenager's reaction. Amy, too, was gifted with a glorious voice. Gracie knew that Amy's dearest hope was one day to perform in opera, should God lead her to the stage. Yet Gracie knew, too, that her young friend would be every bit as delighted to serve in some public school music room.

"Only a child," Gracie whispered. The amazing voice blended youthful lightness and range with qualities generally gained only through extensive musical training.

They moved forward together, rounding the corner of the building, where the neat lawn sloped to a paved arena, dotted with stone benches and loosely roofed, as well as partially walled, with trained grapevines. The singer perched cross-legged on one of the stone benches, her slight body arched toward a woman — surely no older than in her late fifties — who sagged in a wheelchair. The woman wore a loose-sleeved, brightly flowered smock and an emerald green turban; the child's plaid cut-offs and fluorescent pink halter top warred with huge purple terrycloth flowers that confined her sunny hair in straggly ponytails.

The song finished, she spoke in murmurs. The woman remained unresponsive.

"It's okay, Gram," she could be heard to say comfortingly as Gracie and Amy drew closer. "Even when you don't answer, I know you hear me. It was you who taught me all about wishing, how all we have to do is hope hard enough and long enough. . . ." She looked up with a smile. "I'm Lacey Carpenter." She placed a tiny hand in Gracie's. "I'll be ten my next birthday."

"And when is that?" asked Gracie.

The child shrugged. "Not for a while, I guess. I just had one last week."

"Well, happy birthday a week late!" Gracie smiled. "This is Amy Cantrell."

"You're awful pretty."

Amy colored. "So are you, Lacey."

Lacey shrugged. "Maybe someday. Gram always says Mama was beautiful, and that I have her eyes." She sighed, then fastened her open blue gaze on Gracie. "Who are you?"

"Gracie Lynn Parks. Do you mind if we sit with you?"

Lacey ducked her head. "Aunt Kelly says I have the worst manners. Please do join Gram and me." She made a grand gesture. "Aunt Kelly prob'ly wouldn't want me to notice your hair, Gracie, but I can't help it. It's way past *Wow!*" She giggled. "I just noticed that our names rhyme. Gracie and Lacey. Though Aunt Kelly would make me call you Mrs. Parks."

Gracie patted the child's shoulder. "Gracie is fine." She found herself under closer scrutiny.

"It's a good name for you. It sounds like really, really red hair, just like yours, and lots of fun, besides." She leaned forward. "Do you have parakeets?"

11

"Gooseberry wouldn't like that." She added, "Gooseberry is my cat. He prefers his birds outside."

Lacey hid her giggle behind her hand, then said soberly, "Aunt Kelly's allergic to cats." Another sigh shook her frame. "Sometimes I think she's allergic to kids, too."

Amy murmured sympathy.

"Maybe not all kids —" Lacey brightened, "Gram had parakeets, but she didn't have a cat. Do you bake chocolate chip cookies?"

Amy said, "Gracie bakes every kind of cookie you ever thought of! And every single one is delicious."

"And you're invited to come to Gooseberry's house any time you want," Gracie added, "for cookies and lemonade."

"Mmmm." Lacey's expression was rapt. "But I didn't introduce you to Gram!" She caught the woman's limp hand. "Gram, meet Gracie Lynn Parks and Amy —"

"Cantrell," Amy supplied.

"Amy and Gracie, meet Gram. Her other name is Mrs. Gillian Pomeroy. She wasn't always like this. She marched for gun control and 'don't kill animals for their fur' and pollution and stuff like that. But that was before she fell."

"I'm so sorry." Gracie was certain she'd heard the name Gillian Pomeroy somewhere before. But where? "Does your grandmother live near here?"

"Well, she lives *here,* now, of course — but only because she fell, and Aunt Kelly said *she* wasn't into bedpans and stuff, and since it was summer, and I didn't have school, and she could leave her job in Chicago for a little while, and her husband Uncle Grif said she *had* to come —" She snatched a quick breath, then added, "But Gram and me lived in Mason City before she fell."

She leaned against the woman's shoulder. "But it's okay, Gram. I won't let anyone hurt you again. And I'm wishing and wishing, just as hard as ever I can." She peered up at Gracie and Amy. "I know some day Gram'll read stories to me again . . . and tell me what it was like when she was a kid . . . and what it's like to carry picket signs and what Gramps was like. She's going to be all well. Soon. She *has* to. Wishing always, always works! Gram promised."

Gracie bowed her head. *Lord,* she thought, *I could love this sweet child, and know that You already do. Give me the words to say. . . .*

Small, warm hands cupped her face. Gracie looked into wide, earnest eyes.

13

Lacey's voice quavered as she whispered, "You're not sick, too, are you? Like Gram?"

"No, honey. Only praying."

Lacey looked wistful. "Me and Gram always did 'Bless this food' and 'Now I lay me' — but Aunt Kelly says praying's stupid." Her eyes twinkled. "I still do, though, sometimes, when she can't catch me."

Gracie felt she could easily develop a healthy dislike for this Aunt Kelly. She'd have to remind herself that not only did God love even the grumps of the world, He understood fully what had soured them.

Lacey asked, "Is praying almost as good as wishing?"

"Much, much, much better, though I suspect what some people call a 'wish' is truly a prayer. *God* hears and answers prayer."

Lacey wriggled to her knees. "And He listens to kids sometimes, too?"

"He *especially* hears the prayers of children."

Gracie blinked back tears as the child clamped shut both eyes and hands. "Then listen to me, God, okay? I need Gram back. I really *need* her." She paused. "You know Gracie Lynn Parks, right? She says You have to do what kids especially ask. Well, I'll say 'bye now so You can get started."

Now what, Lord? Gracie wondered. *How*

do I convince her that while You do indeed answer prayer, it's often not quite in the ways we ask?

Someone whistled sharply, and a chorus of voices called, "Gracie! Amy!"

Amy said, flustered, "She said ten minutes—"

"We've got to go, dear," Gracie began, then broke off. In the shadows of a nearby grove of aspens, a tall, dark man was watching them intently.

Lacey followed Gracie's glance, and her face hardened. "Uncle Grif," she said coldly. "What's he doing here? He's supposed to still be in Chicago!"

"Gracie!" Paul Meyer, their pastor, hurried toward his errant singers. "Barb's having a panic attack!"

Though Barb's panic attacks were nothing new, Gracie dutifully scrambled to follow. Looking back to smile at Lacey, she noticed that the lurking man had disappeared.

"Gracie! Amy!" Barb did indeed look more apoplectic than usual. "I was afraid the earth had swallowed you up. And what would we have done without our strongest alto and lead soprano? Now . . . *finally!* . . . we can go."

And so they went, chattering in somewhat

hushed voices like a gaggle of fourth-graders.

One end of the retirement community's large public parlor featured a piano, a worn Persian rug in jewel tones with a faded dark blue background, and a more varied assortment of rockers and settees than Gracie had seen anywhere short of a furniture showroom. A crystal vase held flowers cut from the grounds and obviously past their prime, since a small drift of fallen petals littered a white pineapple doily of a vintage Gracie vividly recalled from her grandmother's house.

Less formal was the open room's other end, which offered badminton tables, shuffleboard and a moveable basketball net. Uncle Miltie paused, put his walker in "park" position and aimed an imaginary shot. "Two points!" His crow of triumph was one of boyish delight and Gracie, smiling, could imagine the swishing net, the roar of the crowd. Also known as George Morgan — but only by those who had never winced at his un-funny jokes, so reminiscent of early TV's wildly popular Milton Berle — Uncle Miltie was simply a dear, sweet octogenarian . . . teenager. Gracie had loved just two men more deeply — her late husband Elmo and Arlen, their only son.

Barb marshaled her brood into a semicircle near the piano and — like a pullet nesting — settled herself on the walnut bench. Sheet music rustled; Estelle cleared her throat twice. The breeze ruffling the lace curtains bore the essence of roses while Barb touched the opening chord, allowing them time to find their pitches.

When they swung into a spirited rendition of "Mansion Over the Hilltop," several of the residents nodded and tapped in time as many joined in. There were some in wheelchairs at the edges of the group, and here and there someone had propped a walker or cane. Most, however, moved easily, many even with alacrity, and retained some degree of independence. Only six or so, arranged along one side, were accompanied by attendants. One of these in particular, wearing a bright red baseball cap and, despite the heat, a checked flannel shirt, caught Gracie's attention. His eyes were bright but wandering, and he wore a grin that spoke of mischief.

For some reason, he reminded her of Uncle Miltie. How happy she was that he could live with her! This place was wonderful — but could it ever be "home"? The group's hearty applause and obvious contentment suggested that it was, indeed, home, but with "perks." Here the cares of

17

furnace repairs and lawn upkeep were removed, and a multitude of activities was made available to keep active elders happily involved.

But this man wearing the cap seemed apart from the rest, off in some world of his own. Not an unpleasant world, obviously, but not reality either. *Perhaps better than his reality?* was Gracie's next thought, and then she prayed, *Help us to reach him — all of them — Lord . . . with our music and with Your love.*

And it did seem that he rallied when the choir sang "How Great Thou Art."

During Gracie's favorite arrangement of "The Lord's Prayer," several residents praised with raised hands, and one lithe woman — obviously a dancer — stood up and began to interpret the music with movement and signing. She wore a long, patterned violet dress of unusual design with slit sides and — yes, Gracie determined from a second look — silver ballet slippers.

Barb allowed the choir to be coaxed into more numbers than they'd planned, and Amy Cantrell and Rick Harding sang short solos. Finally the activities director, Blaise Bloomfield, called a halt. "You're insatiable," she reproved. "These people need refreshments, whether you do or not! We'll adjourn to Mason Hall — to munch and mingle."

Pastor Paul adjusted his stride to Gracie's as they left one red brick building and ascended a gently sloping stone walkway bordered with impatiens toward another of similar brick construction. Pausing by the gleaming white columns of the porch, he rested his arm across her shoulder. "This place is a wonderful blessing — not only for the residents, but for their families. They're so alert and active! It's not hard to imagine them, only a few years ago, running across meadows, splashing in streams, falling in love. . . ." He sighed softly. "I have learned so much — so very, very much — from them."

Reaching to touch his arm, she was startled by a sudden volley of shouts from somewhere far behind and to their left. They both turned, and gasped.

"I mention meadows. . . ."

"And there they are, running!" finished Gracie.

And *how* they ran, pausing occasionally to help one another along — gray- and white-haired figures, somewhat miniaturized by distance. Their whoops of exuberance and encouragement seemed wholly joyous, unencumbered by age or — at that moment — by any replaced hips or arthritic knees.

Behind them, their uniformed pursuers

narrowed the space between. Gracie found herself rooting for the escapees.

Pastor Paul chuckled. "I'd heard reports, but it's the first time I've seen Pierre in action."

"Pierre?" The leader of the group, Gracie supposed, the man in the crimson baseball cap. The others had slowed to a dispirited queue, but he sprinted on.

"His real name's Peter, and he's new here. He's not French but he won't answer to anything but Pierre. He was a chef — once. Rather an important one, I gather. His memory's bad, but his spirit's unquenchable." Paul sighed, a semi-sad sigh this time. "He thinks they're holding him back from reporting to work."

"A work he loves," Gracie guessed. She could understand that. Her own love of cooking, of watching others enjoy food her mind had envisioned and her hands had prepared, gave her a greater-than-usual empathy.

One particularly speedy young attendant had reached Pierre. Now, companionably enough to suggest genuine liking, they joined the others, and all made their way back to the lower large brick building. Just at that moment, as she turned away, Gracie caught threads of song. The escapees and staff joined their voices in "How Great Thou Art."

Oh, Lord, Gracie prayed, wiping moisture from her eyes, *don't let me blubber . . . but this is such a wonderful answer to prayer. You did cause us to reach them! You did! You truly are such a great and wonderful God!*

A silver-haired man, dapper in cravat and wingtips despite his wheeled oxygen tank, tapped Gracie's arm with the carved silver lion-head that topped his mahogany cane. "You have such lovely hair, my dear."

She thanked him and — silently — the bottle that periodically replenished her fiery locks.

"Reminds me of sunsets near Kilimanjaro. Could I offer you a lemonade?"

The others were chatting or nibbling cookies, so she moved with him to the refreshment table.

"I recall strapping young natives, glistening like burnished copper, bearing a fresh-killed gazelle suspended from bamboo carrying-poles." He paused, frowning. "Or was it a hammock of palm branches. . . ."

His lengthy pause gave her opportunity to survey the room. Rick Harding was speaking with a young male attendant. Estelle Livett, self-proclaimed diva, accepted

21

homage from three dowagers decked in diamonds. A lavender-haired lady who looked as fragile as Dresden china but moved with chipmunk-swift alacrity patted Amy Cantrell's hand, while her glance roved everywhere — pausing most often, it seemed, on Uncle Miltie. He, meanwhile, had apparently tired of providing comic relief to an appreciative group and was dedicating himself to sampling cookies and discarding each with a grimace.

"I do believe it was the hammock. Yes, indeed it was."

Gracie jerked her attention back to her companion.

"As I was saying, I believe, it was near Everest, and these strapping Sherpas, their faces like burnished bronze, bore fresh-killed goats slung across their shoulders. But the sunrise, my dear — yes . . . yes, very like your hair. . . ." He set his half-empty glass at the back of the table and said, "Do excuse me, my dear, but I think I see the ambassador yonder." Drawing his oxygen tank behind him like Marge Lawrence's Shih Tzu Charlotte on her leash, he made his way to Lester Twomley.

Marge nudged Gracie's elbow. "Such a charming man!" she exclaimed. "I'd scarcely set foot in the door when he absolutely dominated my attention — telling me that I have lovely hair —" she happily fluffed her tresses — "the color of the Ganges at dawn."

Gracie thought she'd heard that the Ganges was a particularly filthy river, but chose not to say so. After all, Marge was her dearest friend and near neighbor — her vanity a cover, Gracie had always felt, for loneliness and insecurity following her divorce.

Marge continued, "And then he told how he and other doctors entered remote mountain villages in India during some epidemic or other, saving literally thousands of lives at the risk of their own." She shuddered. "He never finished his story, and I didn't mind a bit. I was beginning to feel itchy." She picked up a small wedge of sandwich and replaced it. "Then he thought he saw a shah or something and excused himself — but it was only Don Delano. Does Don look like a shah to you, Gracie?"

Gracie answered honestly that as far as she knew she had never seen a shah — but since Don was a science teacher at the local high school, he would probably always look like a high school science teacher to her, even if he turned out to be the long-lost emperor of wherever.

She had the feeling Marge heard none of it, though she nodded rhythmically and murmured a periodic *"Um hmmm."* Her glance dwelt on the silver-haired man — perhaps not exactly a predatory glance, Gracie decided, but certainly an appraising one.

Finally, sighing, Marge said, "He's certainly a well-traveled gentleman."

Or a well-read scoundrel, Gracie thought. *Kilimanjaro, indeed!*

"Did he kiss your hand, Gracie? He did mine." Marge held it to her cheek, her eyes growing dreamy.

Near a looming split-leaf philodendron, Uncle Miltie beat a nervous tattoo with the back legs of his walker — a certain signal that he was anxious to be off. Walking over, Gracie patted his arm. Nearby, the lavender-haired resident was eyeing them curiously.

His stormy expression cleared. "They should have you teach a baking class," he said. "Not a cookie here can measure up to yours — on your worst day."

What a sweet man George Morgan was! He and Aunt Dora had always been Gracie's favorites. Elmo had loved them, too, often shaking his head in fond disbelief at the impractical tricks and un-funny jokes which had earned the nickname Miltie. Both uncle and aunt had been inconsolable at Elmo Parks's sudden death. Without their love and clucking over her, Gracie could scarcely have survived the loss of her dear husband. When Aunt Dora developed inoperable cancer, Gracie reciprocated, promising at her hospital bedside that her husband would have a home with Gracie in Willow Bend as long as she herself had a place to lay her head.

She smiled. What a trio they made, she, Uncle Miltie and Gooseberry, the orange cat who ruled them both — usually with benevolent disdain, though despotism was not unheard of.

"We never did see that beautiful plant," Gracie apologized later, as she and Amy hurried with the others to the parking lot, where Pastor Paul and Blaise Bloomfield waited by the church van.

"No problem. Lacey's more important than any plant." Amy frowned. "Do you think . . . I mean, that man . . ." She sighed. "Do you think he's dangerous?"

"Probably not," Gracie said, though she didn't quite believe that herself. "A child's imagination can be very colorful."

"I remember!" Amy settled back.

Pastor Paul started the ignition, then called from the window, "Now remember, Blaise, this week I'll have the van here a little earlier than usual for your residents who want to attend church but need help getting there."

Fastening her seat belt, Gracie wondered if Pierre would be among them.

2

Sunday morning after Sunday school, the first to climb from the van was Pierre, followed closely by the young attendant who had successfully challenged his recent bid for freedom. Walking side by side, they might have been father and son. Both wore dark suits, pale shirts and equally flamboyant ties, but Pierre now wore an orange-and-blue cap, while the younger man was bare-headed, his straw-colored hair riotous in the sunlight.

Following Blaise Bloomfield, who flashed a cheerful smile at Pastor Paul as he helped her descend the shallow stairs, Gracie counted five others she remembered from the choir visit, including the "dancer," the gentleman who had comandeered both Gracie's and Marge's attention by comparing their hair to elements of nature, and the lady whose lavender tresses were today a dusty rose, a perfect match for her flowing silk ensemble. Not unexpectedly, Eudora McAdoo, as she announced herself, gravitated to Uncle Miltie. His startled expression indicated he might dissolve into one of the rhododendron bushes, given the opportunity.

Gracie's glance sought Rocco Gravino, editor of the *Mason County Gazette*, and found him already observing her. Rocky was a very good friend. He was also an attractive man, with his longish salt-and-pepper hair, his confident stride and the network of crinkling lines at the corners of his eyes when he smiled — as he was doing now, ambling over, offering his arm. She was about to accept when Pastor Paul called out, reminding her that she had a special duty this particular morning.

"What is it, Gracie?" Rocky's brow furrowed. Some accused him of imposing his former big-city tactics on tiny Willow Bend — and Gracie herself had often witnessed him in "veteran-reporter mode." But to those who troubled to look beneath the surface, he was pure marshmallow.

"It's just that Paul asked me to help. With the Scripture."

Rocky shrugged.

A small stone of unhappiness nicked at Gracie's heart. Just a pebble, actually, but a real sadness, nonetheless, that Rocky was so casual in the matter of faith. There were times when she wondered if when he did turn up on Sundays it was only because of her, a thought that always brought self-reproof. She didn't wish to make his regard for her — an obvious affection about which Marge often teased her — seem to be responsible for where he did and didn't go. God had planted a soul-need in him, as in everyone — and whether he was aware of it or not, Rocky was simply responding.

To *God* . . . not to her.

She rushed to explain, "It must sound silly. After all, I read God's Word every day of my life, just not usually aloud — except sometimes to Uncle Miltie. And I've taught Sunday school. It's just that I feel such a . . . *responsibility*, wanting — *needing* — to do it right. Not to let God down." She sighed in confusion. She was saying this badly, making God seem unreasonably demanding and herself infinitely self-absorbed!

"Gracie, dear," Rocky said gently. "You wouldn't know *how* to let God — or *anyone* down! I don't think you even begin to realize how very special you are . . . to how very many people. Now go. I want to hear that wonderful alto from the choir loft." He gave her arm a quick little squeeze.

Gracie wondered why she felt so tense this morning. Her stomach fluttered, her hands trembled so that her sheet music rattled, and Estelle Livett was directing at her strange looks of annoyance or concern. With Estelle, it was hard to tell the difference. Suddenly, Gracie couldn't remember how the anthem began — and yet they'd practiced so thoroughly she'd found herself singing it all week while baking or dusting or doing her daily praise-walk.

She couldn't bring herself to look out over the congregation, as she usually did.

Dear Lord, please don't let me be foolish. I so want, so need, to do my part to Your glory. Please don't allow ego or pride or anything to interfere with my total commitment to You. Amen, she added as Barb's baton commanded the choir's allegiance.

Gracie sighed relief when the few notes of introduction brought the anthem fully to mind.

A good thing, too — since the alto part led with the melody until the refrain. And where the alto section was involved, Gracie was pretty much it. The Turner twins, Tish and Tyne, added volume, but only at her strong leading.

As so often occurred, both words and music spoke to Gracie as though she heard them for the first time, as those in the congregation experienced them.

As Rocky experienced them. *Stop that,* she ordered herself. Still, she found herself singing especially for him — that he might share the deep love she knew for the Savior.

> *Calm our fears, Lord;*
> *Dry our tears, Lord;*
> *Let us sense Your loving presence*
> *   in the pulsing of our blood.*
> *Every day, Lord,*
> *In every way, Lord,*
> *May Your sweet salvation bathe us*
> *   in an ever-flowing flood.*
> *As we sleep, Lord,*
> *When we weep, Lord,*
> *May we bow in acquiescence*
> *   to Your pardoning release.*
> *In this place, Lord,*
> *By Your grace, Lord,*
> *May we rest in firm acceptance*
> *   of Your undergirding peace.*

Gracie experienced a calming within her spirit as soprano and bass sections dominated the refrain . . . as Amy's voice soared in a glorious *obligato* and the anthem closed on an extended Amen. *That's much better, Lord,* she thought, following Lester Twomley as the choir left the loft for seats in the congregation. *Thank you!*

★ ★ ★

Pastor Paul smiled encouragement as he beckoned Gracie to the lectern, then reached to catch her hand as she mounted to the platform. Was it so obvious that she felt unsteady? Now, her heartbeats felt syncopated, a rhythm section in disarray. Her knees shook; she had every expectation that her voice would, as well. She had done this very blessed task often enough before: why did she feel so nervous this morning?

And then her glance fell — by accident — on Rocky, on his nod, his smile, his subtle thumbs-up. *What else do I need, Lord?* she asked within herself. *I've had the reassurance of the anthem, of Pastor Paul's confidence and the encouragement of a dear friend. Best of all, I have You.* She took a deep, steadying breath as Pastor Paul explained to the congregation that he and Gracie would read certain scriptural passages in parts, others in unison.

The silence was such that every slight rustle of clothing, creaking of knees, sigh or whispered remonstrance of parent to child reverberated through the sanctuary, as these members of Gracie's church family listened attentively to the interaction of two voices and God's Holy Word. She felt a surge of love, and breathed a prayer for all of them.

Every week, juice, cookies or rolls, coffee and tea — perhaps hot chocolate in the colder months — were served following church. This particular morning, rolls and doughnuts appeared anonymously — but the fact that they were delivered by Pastor Paul's favorite doughnut shop in Mason City somehow diminished the air of mystery.

"And Gracie," he asked, "would you cut this lemon-poppyseed loaf someone left at the parsonage?" He grinned. He knew as well as she who had left it.

Carefully, she made the first incision.

"Must have it!" A hand gripped her wrist. "You *will* sell it to me!" Pierre's face, his voice, even his physical bearing spoke intensity.

Concentration shattered, she simply stared. He shook her arm. "The bread! I need it!"

She gasped, "The whole loaf? But —"

"Not the loaf, you idiot!" His voice was rising, and people who had been chatting stilled and shifted. "I buy the recipe! Exclusive rights! One million dollars!"

Releasing her at last, he fumbled for his wallet, with trembling hands opened it and extracted a sheaf of bills.

My goodness, it's play money, Gracie realized, her concern evaporating in compassion. "Later, Pierre," she promised, forcing a smile. "See me later."

Pausing only briefly, grumbling only slightly, he moved on.

Her cake slices had never been more raggedy.

Still, during the period of sharing food and fellowship, her emotions settled.

Again.

A hand touched her shoulder.

Pastor Paul. "See what you make of this," he said, and made a *shhh*ing gesture to his lips.

Stepping to one side, she unfolded a four-by-six index card bearing a verse printed in childlike capitals, but only an exceptional child could have composed the text:

HOW MANY SMILES DO I RECORD?
HOW MANY CRIES AND COOS?
HOW MANY PARENTS' PROUD
   EMBRACES?
WHAT A SAD THING TO LOSE!
RANSOM: A LOLLIPOP FOR EVERY
   CHILD IN CHURCH NEXT SUN-
   DAY.

A riddle? In church? But who? And why? And, just as importantly, *what?*

Beyond the open doors, birds sang, children laughed, engines roared to life. Beyond the doors, sunshine waited. Perhaps more importantly, Rocky waited — with the promise of a comfortable Sunday dinner . . . a promise of *normality*.

What's happening here, anyway, Lord? For someone my age, a deeply emotional service might be enough for one morning. But a cryptic note . . . on the heels of a delusional demand for a recipe —

She broke off, remembering. *Pierre!*

At her elbow, Pastor Paul said gently, "He's forgotten, for now. He's already on the van. But later — this afternoon — we need to talk about this." He tapped the note.

She nodded, numbly grateful for the reprieve. *Still, Lord. I feel like I'm on an emotional roller coaster. Could You prescribe some spiritual tranquilizer?*

Immediately, "Let not your heart be troubled" came to mind.

Gracie sipped her iced tea, took another bite of her scrambled eggs and knew that things would work out. After all, God and the members of the Eternal Hope Choir — with the assistance of Uncle Miltie, Rocky — and Gooseberry, of course — had unraveled mysteries much knottier than a note demanding lollipops. Only her imagination at its most overactive would equate sugary candy with some sinister threat.

"Let not your heart be troubled" applied as fully to worrywart disciples in polyester-cotton blends as it had when Jesus first spoke the calming words so long ago. *Help me to remember that, Lord,* she prayed in her thoughts. *I get so fussed up at times, so concerned and confused — forgetting that such turmoil proves a faltering faith.* She drew a deep sigh and smiled at Rocky, who was waging a losing battle with his reuben sandwich.

Surrendering for the moment, he asked, "Feeling better, my friend?"

"Abe's Sunday lunches have great curative powers." *So does prayer,* she thought. Why didn't she say it aloud? And then the moment was past. She chided herself.

"Could we talk about it?" He glanced at his watch.

He had said, in the church parking lot, that they'd have to take separate cars to Abe Wasserman's deli. Just as well, since Pastor Paul would be expecting her to return soon.

"When do you need to be at the office?"

"Not for nearly an hour. Besides, your concern for my schedule sounds like avoidance." He reached to cover her hand briefly with his.

How comforting the connection of hands could be! El had always been able to make her world right so quickly with that simple gesture of affection.

"Talk," Rocky encouraged. He'd enlisted his fork in the War of Straying Sauerkraut.

When she'd given the details of the note — what few there were — and showed him the verse, he asked, "A joke?"

"Maybe." She broke off a bit of Abe's toasted poppy-seed rye and watched butter melt into the crevices. "That depends."

"Depends on. . . ." Rocky's voice was suspended.

"On what's missing. If anything. And if other demands follow."

"Lollipops for the children —"

"Sound harmless?"

"Ye-e-es." He managed to drag the word to three syllables. "Don't they?"

"What would happen, do you think, if we don't comply?"

He seemed to be struggling with a smile. "If you don't give them lollipops?"

"If we call their bluff." She savored a bite of overtoasted crust. "Not the children's. The . . . thief's."

She could almost hear El saying, *Gracie,*

dear, this isn't Cold War intrigue, you know. We're talking lollipops here, not nuclear secrets.

"I know it sounds silly," she said. "It *will* be silly if this is a one-time thing. But it may not be. This could be a 'testing of the water,' to see how compliant we're willing to be."

"Lollipops now, the deed to the church later?"

"Or something else we'd find it hard to grant."

"Like . . ."

She shrugged. "Like supporting a cause we don't really believe in. Like weakening our principles in any of a hundred ways."

"But you wouldn't!"

Oh, how she wished he'd used the pronoun *we!*

"That's right. But — you've heard about the frog and the boiling water?"

He laughed. "I believe your esteemed minister used the example in a sermon not long ago."

Despite the hint of sarcasm in the word *esteemed,* she felt a flush of pleasure. *So he really is listening, Lord! Thank You!* "Perhaps someone decided to experiment."

"See just how far they could push?"

"This could be a test. One we can't study for. But," she finished slowly, "one we'll certainly pray about."

His hand had found hers again. "I know you will, Gracie. And if I hear anything, I'll let you know. Although it seems unlikely."

Smiling, she tried to picture clues to a lollipop mystery arriving at the newspaper office in an unmarked envelope.

"Eat up!" he commanded, as he rolled up his shirt sleeves, and renewed his own battle.

When only a few diners remained, Abe came to join them at their table. With him, he brought a frosty half-pitcher of iced tea and a glass for himself. Without asking, he replenished Gracie's drink — but Rocky shook his head. "I'm sorry, Abe, but I hear the presses calling."

Abe smiled. "Too much business, dear friend, is like an overabundance of vinegar in the dressing. Balance is all."

Rocky shrugged. "And there are days when balance is harder to come by than true friendship, of which I have a fine supply. Forgive me."

Abe waved him away. "How could I feel insulted when you leave me in sole possession of our delightful Gracie's company?"

Gracie chided, "Enough! You'd turn anyone's head with such flattery!"

"Does a newspaperman have sufficient words to explain the difference between flattery and sincerity?"

"Not in this case, I'm afraid." Rocky squeezed Gracie's shoulder. He winked, and strode out.

Abe threw back his head and chuckled heartily. He poured his tea to the tinkling of ice cubes. "Now, Gracie, what is this latest problem that clouds your pretty eyes?"

When she had shown the message and explained its appearance, he said soberly, "To steal from God's house —" He shook his head. "And you have no idea what has been taken?"

"Not yet. Obviously something from the children's rooms. Pastor Paul asked that I meet him . . . later." She consulted her watch. "Soon."

"Coos. Cries. The nursery?"

Nodding, she mentally inventoried the contents of the sunny room where small children were rocked, entertained and loved while their parents concentrated on the service. Cribs, rocking chairs, playpens — all too large for anyone to spirit away. "A toy perhaps?"

"And yet the word *record* would suggest —"

"A mirror, then? There's a small one

framed with brightly colored animals, a Noah's ark in the lower right corner —"

Arlen had loved it when he was small, and Gracie had watched dozens of other infants and toddlers cooing at it, reaching to touch the engraved giraffes or elephants or trace the arc of the rainbow. The silvering was a bit worn off now, the image clouded and imperfect, but the emotional value of the gift and the memories it summoned were incalculable.

"A mirror does record, yes," Abe agreed, "though briefly. How large is this mirror?"

Gracie measured with her hands.

"Small enough."

Gracie sighed with anticipated grief.

"And there is nothing else?"

Her nod had already begun when a chilling thought struck.

The cradle roll — the record of all the little ones who had been born into and grown up at Eternal Hope!

Surely not that fragile document — some inscriptions older by decades than Gracie. So many names there had long been listed in Heaven. *Dear Lord, please no.* . . .

"And this . . . 'ransom'?" Abe asked without smiling. "You will pay it?"

Gracie shifted uneasily. *If it were the cradle roll.* . . .

41

"The story is told of a man who asked his neighbor for a fig from his tree. The neighbor gave it gladly. 'But see,' the man said, 'how the branch bows with the fruit! And you have so much. Perhaps you could give me the branch. I believe your tree would be better for the pruning.' The neighbor hesitated, then with his pruning shears prepared to sever the branch. 'Only wait!' the man commanded. 'My branch represents at least a fifth of the tree. It hangs quite close to my own property. Indeed, in some future years, it may crowd our boundary! What a shame to separate this branch from its fellows! Only see how many trees you would have still remaining. Surely, for friendship's sake — and since you are a generous man — you could spare this one small tree and the tiny spot of earth its roots involve. . . .' " Abe's voice died away, and he shrugged expressively.

"And before long," Gracie guessed, "the whole orchard was appropriated."

"Lollipops for the children," Abe agreed, "have something in common with a single fig. Is it not with good reason a government says, 'We do not negotiate with terrorists'? And have our police not often urged that the demands of kidnappers be left unmet?" He turned his glass of untasted tea. "This mirror-napper of yours may be pulling a childish prank which seems innocent, even playful. Or . . ." his voice deepened and darkened, "he may only be very clever, someone with a much larger plan that promises great evil."

And if it had been the enduring, one-of-a-kind cradle roll that was stolen. . . .

Gracie shivered, a dark shadow settling in her heart.

3

The cradle roll hung in its accustomed place. Gracie breathed a deep prayer of gratitude and relief, then confided her fear for its safety to Pastor Paul.

"I scarcely noticed it until now," he admitted, flushing. "And yet to some members here it might be the most important document we own."

"Except for the deed," she said slowly, remembering what Rocky had suggested.

"At least *that's* in a safe place."

Another item that had not crossed Gracie's mind — a quilt recording the names and embroidered hand-shapes of primary and intermediate classes of a decade ago — lay folded neatly in a crib.

Gracie removed a poster hung loosely with masking tape to reveal a light, clean spot on the windowless wall where the mirror had hung. "So I made the right guess in the first place!"

Pastor Paul was at her elbow in an instant.

"The Noah's Ark mirror," she answered his frown.

He sank into one of the totally inadequate miniature chairs. "Gracie, we need to video-tape the church contents. Obviously memory — at least mine — doesn't keep a very good inventory."

"As soon as possible," Gracie agreed. She turned slowly, forefinger to her chin.

"Something else missing?" he asked tensely.

No, it wasn't that. Moving one of the cribs, she pulled out a large rectangular packet wrapped in brown paper. "I never noticed this before. Of course, I don't come here often. Should we . . . ?"

"I think we must," he said, "under the cir-cumstances." He reached for it.

By the time she returned from the kitchen with a paring knife, Paul had slipped off the binding string and laid the wrapping aside, exposing a lovely Beatrix Potter print matted in medium blue and framed in walnut.

"I wonder who contributed this!" she gasped, "and why it hasn't been hung, or at least acknowledged in the bulletin."

"No one has mentioned it to me," Pastor Paul told her as he carefully realigned the wrappings.

"Who could have accepted it?" she asked, even as he said, "Who might know?"

Mentally, she scanned the list of those involved with Christian Education — especially the coordinators for the nursery. Her fellow choir members, the Turner twins and Amy Cantrell, who taught Primary, stayed active with the smaller children's events.

"But they would have mentioned something this exciting!"

Carefully, she replaced the package and adjusted the crib. "Unless —"

He leaned forward, and her fears for the tiny chair in which he perched increased. "I know that look, I'm afraid."

She hugged herself against a sudden chill. Excitement, she suspected. "You don't suppose the . . . *thief* . . . left it!"

He gave her a quizzical look. "What kind of thief —"

"Exactly!" She made a gingerly attempt at one of the chairs herself, but quickly switched to the edge of a table marked with crayon scribbles. "What if this . . . person . . . doesn't feel comfortable with outright thievery, and so makes it an . . . exchange?" She was expressing the ridiculous thoughts even as they entered her mind.

"The motivation being — ?" His tone suggested temporary sanity was an issue.

As indeed it might be. She shrugged. "Someone wanting attention?"

"A young person?"

She hoped not one they knew!

He sighed cavernously. "What do we do, Gracie?"

"All we *can* do is wait. See what happens next."

"And the . . . ransom?"

"I don't think we should pay it."

"Even lollipops?"

"Even lollipops."

He managed a smile. "I'm sure the children would disagree. But yes, we need to make a point right at the start."

"And I suppose we must lock the church — even in the daytime." *How this must grieve You, Lord, when Your house is closed against those who need You most.*

"I — can't do that, Gracie. I'll watch as much as I can, and ask that others do the same. But we'll lock up at night. Even that bothers me." He stood, and the little chair rocked.

In relief, Gracie supposed. It hadn't been designed for such a lanky burden.

Uncle Miltie and Gooseberry, both looking contented, napped on their respective perches. Suspecting as much, Gracie tiptoed into the kitchen. Gooseberry's bowl had been licked clean, and since the stove proved that Uncle Miltie had prepared eggs and bacon, she was reassured that both were well-fed. When he had first come to live with her, Gracie had made certain that meals were prepared three times a day. But after a week, Uncle Miltie insisted, "I came to share your life, not take it over. You need some time to yourself, as we all do." As her friendship with Rocky developed, Uncle Miltie had been even more adamant. "All the years of our marriage, Doris and I snacked Sunday noon — unless company was coming."

Remembering sumptuous spreads of fried chicken, mashed potatoes, homemade rolls, flawless gravy, angel food cake and a proliferation of salads, relishes and spreads, Gracie — a bit wounded — asked, "Then you considered El and me company?"

"The very best kind," he had assured her with a hug. "Company, family *and* our very favorite people."

Smiling, and — not surprisingly — blinking back a tear, Gracie refrigerated the half-dozen eggs and tub of butter, threw the empty bacon package into the garbage, washed and dried the skillet and few dishes and cleaned the stove top. Then, going upstairs, she changed from her church clothes into walking shirt and denims and laced up her shoes. It was difficult, Sunday mornings, to fit in a praise-walk before Sunday school. But there was something particularly satisfying about walking through a Sunday afternoon, music cassette disengaged while she paused to spend a few moments with people often too busy during the week to chat. Of course, that was different from talking at length with God — Who was never too busy.

Passing Cordelia Fountain's tourist home, Gracie was surprised to see Lacey Carpenter draped into a tire swing and hanging lazily off a tree branch. Spotting Gracie, she thumped to the ground and called out a delighted, "Gracie!"

Gracie waited for the child to catch her breath.

"I've been praying and praying and *praying!*" she said. "If God's listening at all, He has to hear me — but I haven't heard anything back yet." She sighed noisily.

"Would your aunt mind if you walked with me a bit?"

"She's not even home." Lacey giggled. "Well, of *course* she's not home! That's back in Chicago! We're just here for the summer."

Gracie adjusted her pace to Lacey's, although she made no effort to imitate the girl's variations. These included walking for a time along the top of a brick edging, arms extended for balance, and carefully avoiding all sidewalk cracks, while hopscotching over petals blown from roses past their prime. "Then she's visiting friends?" Gracie wondered why she hadn't taken her niece along.

Lacey shrugged. "She just said if she wasn't back for supper to get myself something from the fridge. Oh — *and* told me not to leave the yard."

They were well beyond that now.

"Don't worry, Gracie. She'd love it if somebody'd kidnap me." She giggled. "I wish *you* would! You and Gooseberry."

"Why don't we go back and sit on the porch?"

Lacey propped her hands on her hips. "Are you afraid of Aunt Kelly?" she demanded.

"Not afraid of her, dear. I just don't want to go against her wishes. She *is* your guardian, isn't she?"

"Until Gram gets better, I guess." She was obviously pouting. Still, she turned and followed Gracie to the large porch swing, one of many features that made the historic tourist home so inviting. The seat was too high for Lacey to sit normally, so she lay on her stomach, looked up into Gracie's face, and shoved the swing erratically back and forth.

Gracie thought she knew how a whale must feel in a hurricane.

"How will God answer me anyway? I don't suppose He has a phone."

"He speaks to people in different ways," Gracie said thoughtfully. "I never hear a voice at all —"

"Then how do you know it's *God?*"

"This sounds like a non-answer . . . but there are times when I just *know* — by the way things turn out."

Lacey frowned.

"Like with your grandmother," Gracie explained. "If you prayed for her to show she heard you, and she squeezed your hand."

"Ohhhhhh!" Lacey's blue eyes widened. "But she *did!* And Aunt Kelly said," she primped her mouth and snapped in a sharp voice, " 'Don't be foolish! It's only a twitch!' " She crawled backwards onto the swing and allowed Gracie to pump. "But it really was Gram! I knew it! And maybe it was . . . *God,* too? Do you think?" She snuggled into the crook of Gracie's arm.

Gracie hugged her close. How long it had been since she'd held a child like this! Suddenly, she yearned for a visit from her grandson, little Elmo.

"Do you?"

"Dear child, you can be certain that God was caring about you — and about your grandmother."

" 'Course it was before I'd prayed yet."

"He knows our needs before we do."

"He sounds awful nice!" She snuggled closer.

Silently, Gracie prayed for the child, for her grandmother, even for Aunt Kelly.

Lacey straightened, pitching the swing. "We could go have cookies with Gooseberry!"

"We aren't to leave the yard."

Lacey sighed. "If I hadn't told you, we could."

"Lacey . . ."

"I know. I know." She hopped off the swing and did deep bends at the top of the porch steps. "Aunt Kelly's a pain."

"Lacey —"

"I guess God wouldn't like that."

"I guess you're right."

"But if I take it back He'll still listen to me?"

Lord, give me the words to lead her to an un-

derstanding of You, she prayed, then coaxed Lacey back beside her and began — quietly and gently — to teach her.

Gracie had set the alarm for 5:30, but woke before it sounded. For several minutes she lay still, listening to Gooseberry's motorized purring and reviewing what she knew of the day's events. The praise-walk was a given, especially since yesterday's hadn't materialized, even late. She planned to end at the church, and hoped the Finkmeyer great-grandchildren wouldn't lose confidence in their caterer simply because she wore her exercise clothes and walking shoes.

They had to go over the final checklist for Wednesday evening. *Lord, I can scarcely imagine — sixty years of marriage! How many memories — both good and bad — have crowded those years. Triumphs and tragedies . . . births and deaths . . . times when they were ecstatically in love, and those others when they wondered how they could ever have imagined they were meant for one another. But through it all, Lord, Your love brought meaning to the pieces and produced a glorious whole.*

She realized that her thinking had turned to her own marriage, hers and El's. She couldn't speak for the Finkmeyers but she felt they knew, as she did, that keeping a marriage together so long surely required real character and love. Perhaps what had been true for El and Gracie applied to any marriage that worked. That lasted. *Oh, Lord, ours ended much, much too soon.* . . .

Would she ever fully recover from her sadness at the suddennness, the completeness of her loss?

Gooseberry awoke as she dressed. "What do you think, Gooseberry? The green sweatsuit or the brown?" It seemed obvious that Gooseberry preferred the green — which Rocky had also complimented on several occasions. She wondered if she might possibly see Rocky — exercising his dogs, or perhaps driving early to the newspaper office. She had to admit that she didn't look bad for an old gal. All greens, ranging from the palest mint to the deepest evergreen, dramatized the particular shade of her hair — only a few tones off, actually, from Gooseberry's pumpkin hue.

As they went downstairs together, Uncle Miltie turned away from the refrigerator, a half-gallon milk jug tilting precariously. "Got a riddle for you, Gracie!"

Gracie resisted the urge to groan. Uncle Miltie's routine jokes were always bad enough! But with yesterday's theft of the nursery mirror, she wasn't certain she needed any more riddles just then.

He poured milk on cereal sprinkled lavishly with blueberries. "How would you describe the difference between Gooseberry and a pumpkin?" Carefully, he set down the milk, plunked himself into a chair and regarded her with bright, expectant eyes.

Whatever she answered would be wrong. If she said that Gooseberry was the more pumpkin-colored of the two, he'd say —

Who knew what he'd say?

Never taking his gaze from her, he chewed a bite slowly. Then another. "I'm disappointed in you, Gracie," he said at last. "If you can't tell the difference, I'd better hide Gooseberry when it comes jack-o-lantern time!" He threw back his head and chortled heartily.

Gooseberry shuddered. Gracie shook her head. She threw her uncle a fond look, anyway. There were many worse faults than telling unfunny jokes. Just at the moment, though, she was having a hard time thinking of any.

Breathing deeply, doing a few stretches — while Gooseberry performed his own sinuous feline version — Gracie set off briskly. Her arms moved with exaggerated energy, as though preparing for flight; his marvelous tail, aloft, waved majestically. It was the kind of morning she loved, still a bit cool, misty enough to add a sense of mystery to low-lying spots they passed. In her ears piped an ornate adaptation of "Crown Him with Many Crowns" by Michael Faircloth, one of her favorite pianists. She'd heard him in person once, at a retreat for married couples along Chesapeake Bay. She amended her thought gently. She and dear El had heard him in concert. She remembered their walking together the length of the pier, sitting on a wooden bench while sunset faded and the water murmured its soothing repetition, splashing rhythmically against the pilings.

"Amazing." She'd rested against El's shoulder, his left arm encircling her. "Water never stops." *Like our love,* her thoughts continued. "Ever since God set it in motion, it's moved as He planned." Storms might whip the waves to fury, but they could never dissuade nature from following His plan.

Remembering now, she prayed against a tender background of "Amazing Grace." *Lord, if only we could be as obedient to Your leading as the waves are, and the seasons, and even the birds and animals. They never rebel, never try to carve an independent way. Some-*

times, it isn't that we don't want *to follow, it's just that we can't discern among the many directions that tug us. So we can't be quite certain which is Your voice, what is Your will. Make it clear to us, Lord. Show us the best way to go. And especially, speak to Your child Lacey, and — if it is Your will — reunite her with the Gram she remembers and loves. Amen.*

It was a temptation to ask that Uncle Miltie be granted a more carefully edited sense of humor — but without his light-hearted tricks and unskilled jokes, he simply wouldn't be the Uncle Miltie she knew and loved.

"We can handle it, can't we, Gooseberry?" she asked, and the cat perked up his ears — in the affirmative, she truly believed. They had reached their regular turning place, and now Gooseberry paused, remonstrating audibly as she continued toward Eternal Hope Church. "We need to tend to business, Gooseberry," she soothed. But he seemed unconvinced — even, she thought, a bit huffy.

Eventually, without even a good-bye nod or meow, he took the "correct" path.

Gracie smiled. Despite what she'd said about animals in her prayer, there were still those who expressed a stubborn independence!

★ ★ ★

The church was still, and one would have thought, should have been utterly quiet. But there were those shifting, settling sounds any building breathes — or was it more than that? Hesitating, she listened so closely her ears vibrated with the silence. Nothing.

And then a door closed — its stealth more jarring than a slam could possibly have been. So early? Perhaps Pastor Paul — unlocking the doors. Or someone who lived closer to the church had discharged the duty on his or her way to work.

By the time Gracie reached the entrance leading to the parking lot, the noise of an engine was fading, its vehicle no longer visible.

Now what?

Now *who?*

It couldn't have been the Finkmeyers, here and gone, for, after all, she was early.

Early enough, she decided, to look around. Perhaps the "exchange-thief" had suffered an attack of conscience and returned the mirror! Curious to see if the Beatrix Potter print was still there, in any event, Gracie hurried to the nursery, her heart pounding as it never did on her lengthy, vigorous walks.

No, the print still rested on the floor,

waiting, and the rectangle of wall showed clean and empty.

Well . . . not quite empty. A pink four-by-six index card was taped in its center. Not wanting to tamper with evidence, she left it where it was, but since it was posted upside down — for what strange reason? — it made for difficult reading.

I AM ONE WHERE ONCE WERE
   TWO . . .
HEAVY, ROUND, OF GOLDEN HUE
PASSED TO PEOPLE, PEW ON
   PEW . . .
AMAZING WHAT MY CONTENTS
   DO!

HELD FOR RANSOM, WHO KNOWS
   WHY?
WILL SOMEONE FIND ME, BY
   AND BY?

RANSOM: FOR THE ALTAR, A
   BOUQUET OF MONEY PLANT
   AND RED CARNATIONS.

These clues were certainly less subtle than those in the first note, thought Gracie, as she hurried to the sanctuary. Even from the rear, she could see that one offering plate was indeed missing. The space wasn't completely vacant, however. Curious, she moved forward. The scant morning light from the stained-glass windows reflected from . . . plastic? A plastic bundle tied with gold crinkle-tie that curled into ringlets that cascaded over the front and edge of the altar cloth.

A plastic bundle of . . . *lollipops!*

4

"And so," Abe said, relaxing at a corner table of his deli with Gracie and Rocky, "we now have a thief who pays his own ransom."

"So it seems." Gracie sighed.

"Though if you continue, distributing the ransom as required. . . . ?"

"We might as well have bought the lollipops ourselves —" She broke off. "Does this sound as silly to you as it does to me?"

Amy Cantrell arrived with their drinks. "Would it help if *I* gave them to the children?" she asked earnestly. "Since I'm still a kid, sort of — it might satisfy . . . whoever's doing this, but it wouldn't be like —" She hugged the empty tray. "Though maybe not."

Abe pulled out a chair for her. "Sit with us, my dear. Let me tell you a story."

Amy obeyed with alacrity. "I love his stories!" she confided to Gracie. "I've been writing them into my journal —" she flushed. "Is that all right with you, Mr. Wasserman?"

He raised his hands, palms up. "I shall be immortalized in the annals of literature!" he crowed. "That fame should occur to such a one as I!"

Amy blushed. "He teases like that all the time."

And she loves it, Gracie knew.

Abe took a sip of black coffee. Rocky sat back in his chair, a small smile warming his expression.

Not the steely-eyed newspaperman today, Gracie thought. *Just a man relaxing with friends.*

"There was, in a small village in ancient Israel, a man, a councilman, let's say, who conceived in his own mind that he would remain detached from any results of his decisions. He would watch carefully. If the people were pleased, saying that the decision was a good one, with quite positive results, he would spread abroad the word that he had been its author, and so ride triumphantly on a tide of public approval. But if the results proved negative, perhaps even damaging, or at some point disastrous, certain lieutenants would publish the news that someone else — an enemy, perhaps even a secret insurrectionist within their own midst — had done this thing to undermine the people's confidence in their leader. His lieutenants would scurry everywhere, apparently seeking to unearth this villain. Since the councilman really wished no harm to anyone, the insurrectionist would never be discovered. And after a period of unrest, things would go on as before."

Abe paused, sipping more coffee.

Allowing what he's said so far to soak in, Gracie thought, *giving us time to apply the story to us.* She turned to God with the question, *Are we, the church, the councilman — wanting always to seem right?* She squirmed a bit in her chair.

Abe continued, "But there came a time when he could make no decision. It seemed a small affair — but one with broad implications. The king of a neighboring kingdom sent a gift, but this was a king who had often threatened war, and there seemed no reason for appeasement on his part. After all, he had thousands of troops at his disposal — a hundred iron chariots and weapons forged in fire. The village was poor and unprotected, its only weapons the stones that littered its fields and composed its homes. Why had this powerful king sent a gift to an obscure village? Should the councilman accept it? And if so, to enrich himself, or to be shared with all of the villagers? It was impossible to tell what lay within the wrappings. It might be of great value. Or —" Abe paused dramatically — "it might contain poisonous snakes, or some gaseous substance that would make the hair and teeth fall out."

Amy quieted her giggles with apparent effort.

Abe regarded his part-time employee fondly. "In that event," he said, "the wrappings might contain old age — a gift we will discuss at some future time. We are all much too young to consider that now." He waited for the general laughter to subside before continuing.

"The councilman was in a quandary. Should he even accept the gift? Would it ingratiate him with this king? Would some future service be required as a result of acceptance? But if he spurned the gift — then what? Might not the king send out his troops in anger to lay waste to the village . . . perhaps to execute the councilman himself? But there was a third alternative. Do nothing. Allow the gift to lie unclaimed." Again he paused, sipped coffee, and pushed back his chair.

"But —" protested Amy, "wouldn't that be as bad as rejecting it?"

"Perhaps."

"And the king might still —"

"He might . . . or he might not. He might consider that the councilman felt himself unworthy to receive a gift from such a great personage as the king himself. Or, again — he might consider it the ultimate arrogance, and want to kill the councilman not once, but twice. And there is, of course, the possibility that the gift might do its damage, if neither accepted nor rejected. Suppose it contains a poisoned delicacy. As animals rip away the wrappers and consume the contents, perhaps that poison will be spread throughout the entire countryside."

Amy gasped. "You think the lollipops might be poisoned?"

"Dear child, there were no lollipops in ancient Israel."

She flushed.

Gracie patted her hand. It was easy, when Abe spun a story, to forget where fable began and fact left off.

"Again, the gift might be something highly desirable — jewels, perhaps, or many talents of gold. Nothing corrupts the human heart like great wealth. Perhaps the king was counting on that — if not with the councilman, with someone who would ultimately betray him." Abe stood, pushing in his chair and leaning on its back. "Or the gift may contain scorpions, which — as the box deteriorates, will scatter into the land, afflicting its citizens."

Amy stood, accusing, "You're not going to finish the story, are you!"

"The story is like life. We never know how one thing leads to another."

The door swished open, admitting new customers.

Amy said, "*That* is *so* unfair!"

"Ah . . . then this one fable will not be recorded in your journal?"

She began slowly, "I'll have to include it . . . but I'll give it an ending!"

"And what ending will you give it, sweet Amy?"

She frowned, hugging the tray again. "I don't know. I suppose I'll just have to wait and see what happens."

"With the unopened gift?"

She spoke over her shoulder as she moved to the table where the customers were now seated. "With the lollipops, I guess."

"And I, too, must be off," Abe said, "tending to my business — which includes your own order, dear friends!" He shook his head. "I only pray that any dilemmas of food and drink and service that confront me today are much less weighty than decisions you must make in this matter."

Alone, Gracie and Rocky sat in silence for

a time. *What a strange silence, Lord,* she con-fided, *comfortable because I have learned con-tentment with this friend, yet agitated by a situation Abe has made only more complex. Or is that unfair? Abe himself hasn't added to the problem but has merely exposed its many danger spots.*

"What will you do?" Rocky asked, making overlapping wet glassprints on the tabletop.

She answered honestly, "I have no idea."

"Abe made some valid — though convo-luted — points."

"Somewhat difficult to apply to lolli-pops."

"The poison? The wealth? True. But the ramifications —"

Amy approached with their order.

"For now," Gracie said, "I choose the 'do nothing' option. My most important deci-sion at the moment will be, do I eat my fries with my fork — or my fingers?"

The festive package of lollipops had been moved from the altar to the communion rail. Displacing its waterfall of crinkle-tie, Barb reached behind the rail to reclaim the collapsible metal music stand used only when the choir sang a cappella — or when difficult accompaniment demanded her total attention and she enlisted Gracie as co-conductor. A little rusty and more than a little wobbly, the stand had barely survived the abuse of Les Twomley's childhood trumpet practice and had long been there on permanent loan.

"I could hear the other kids running bases whenever I had to practice," he said. "I was convinced Mom left the window open to intensify my suffering." He chuckled. "Probably just wanted to give the noise another direction to go."

Gracie waited for his next predictable line.

"I never *did* play reveille those years in the army —"

"Well, look at this!" Barb interrupted, before Les could finish with an apology to his dear, departed, long-suffering — and surely disillusioned — parents.

A blast of reflected light assaulted Gracie's eyes. The Turner twins gasped in unison, and Estelle Livett emitted a soprano shriek, her trademark tremulo intact.

Barb deflected the glare. "Ark and animals all accounted for!"

The nursery mirror — returned!

"How strange. . . ."

Strange, certainly, but Gracie breathed relief. A pattern of theft-replace-*and-return* had been set. If she'd had any doubt that the offering plate would reappear, this dispelled it.

"Shouldn't we dust it for fingerprints, or something?" asked Estelle. "Not that it would do any good *now*."

Quickly, Barb set the mirror on the front pew and wiped both hands down the sides of her long shirt.

Amy Cantrell asked gently, "Does it matter, anyway, who sto— er, took it? Now that it's back?"

Apparently Estelle had watched enough detective shows to understand such things. "Of course it matters! They could sort of — separate Barb's prints . . . maybe find a — a — little piece of one that isn't hers —"

"A partial," Don Delano supplied.

Estelle failed to look grateful. "I was going to say that! *Partial*."

"Besides, no harm's done." Amy's lovely face glowed with hope. "Right? Everything will be returned?"

"Of course, dear," Gracie assured. "Soon, I'm sure."

Rick Harding, who seldom grumbled, grumbled. "In the meantime, it'll be hard taking up a collection." Obviously, he was on the ushering team for the month.

The anthem demanded full concentration. Its arrangement was hauntingly ornate, and Gracie liked the words. *They don't allow us to hide behind the "we," Lord. Each of us feels an individual guilt . . . but also a personal worth in Your eyes.*

The piano introduction completed, they began fumblingly:

> *Weighted by sins I have committed*
> *against Your love, against Your law,*
> *I come, imperfectly submitted,*
> *admitting every fault and flaw.*

Estelle's "mezzo-squawk," as Uncle Miltie termed it in his less charitable moods, sailed into unexplored space, and the Turner twins seemed to experience identical spasms; however, Barb at the piano — and Gracie and her baton — plodded on.

> *Repentantly, upon my knees,*
> *dispelling doubting and unease,*
> *I seek release,*
> *Your gentle peace*
> *to heal my soul-wounds, deep and raw.*

Les collapsed to his chair, hands over his ears. Perhaps, Gracie thought, this exceeded any damage even his trumpet had wrought.

Only Rick Harding and Amy Cantrell endured, wholly on key.

Encouraged, cleansed, I reach to take
Your precious blood, erasing stain,
Your body, broken for my sake —
converting pain and loss to gain!

The final chord signaled a flurry of groans and complaints. Marge Lawrence grimaced.

"Too high for me!"

"Too low."

"When are we doing it? Not next week, I hope!"

"Let Rick and Amy do it as a duet!"

"And maybe Gracie. Why weren't you *singing,* Gracie?"

"Where did you find it, Barb?" Marybeth Bower wanted to know.

"What's wrong with sticking to what we *know?*"

Barb seemed unperturbed. "You'll learn it in no time," she said with apparent confidence. "And then one Sunday you'll do a marvelous job with it. Just as you always do!" She closed the music stand with such finality that a part jarred loose and clattered against the railing.

"Oh, dear!"

"Used to do that all the time," Les Twomley comforted. "Got any transparent tape?"

71

★ ★ ★

Gracie surveyed Eternal Hope's family activity center, now decked for celebration. An easel held a large collage of photographs — the earliest black and white — with a four-inch iridescent "60" at each corner of the display. Streamers crisscrossing the ceiling swayed slightly in fan-produced breezes that incited hundreds of helium-filled balloons to wobbling migration. White linen draped the elongated buffet table, as well as round tables for eight, placed to allow space for comfortable passage — even for guests of the most generous proportions.

By the time the Finkmeyer grandchildren arrived with the guests of honor, everything had long been in readiness. Tapers glowed, place settings gleamed, warming pans steamed. Flushed and frail, Lorenzo and Sadie Finkmeyer clutched one another's arthritic hands. They seemed to require that mutual support. Hallie, Lorenzo's sister-in-law, fluttered nervously behind them. Two toddlers, eluding their mother's grasp, rolled on the floor, jealous of the attention diverted from themselves.

Lord, Gracie thought, as she watched the guests of honor, *how often in sixty years they must have leaned on one another's under-*

standing and love! Did they come to You, as well, in times of anxiety and loss?

Yet this should be a time of joy, a time to absorb the affection and respect of those around them, to exult in six decades of triumphs! Instead, both look as though they'd rather be anywhere but here, basking in compliments and hugs.

One young woman, daring in black silk, said unnecessarily, "These are our grandparents."

Sadie nodded stiffly. "I'd feel ever so much more at home if I could've brought my apron."

"Wears it all the time," her husband said fondly, "with me firmly anchored by the strings."

"One of these times I'll forget — knot them around your neck!"

Sadie seemed startled when others laughed. The teasing, Gracie realized, had been meant for him alone.

When they were barely beyond hearing, Marge Lawrence turned from the warming oven where she'd just placed a tray of rolls. "Aren't they sweet? I'll bet when they were in third or fourth grade, he even dipped her pigtails in his inkwell."

"Not possible," muttered Uncle Miltie, as he ran steaming water into the sink.

Marge bristled. "They were, too, using inkwells then!"

"Sure were."

"Even when my older brother —" She broke off, holding a butter knife aloft. "You agree with me?"

"Nope."

"Then —"

"His name begins with 'F'," he explained cryptically.

When he said nothing further, when all work seemed suspended in expectancy, Gracie suggested, "Later? Are the relish trays ready?"

The Turner twins replied in tandem affirmation.

"And the canapes?"

"Aye, aye, Captain!" Barb saluted smartly.

Uncle Miltie snorted, and Marge muttered, "Whatever the alphabet has to do with inkwells!" before turning her attention to miniature sticky buns.

Passing quietly among the guests with trays of appetizers and replenishing iced fruit punch, Gracie gleaned bits of information about the anniversary pair. Sadie Ellen Newcomb had graduated from a state teachers' college in faraway Pennsylvania, moved to Indiana to board with an ailing uncle and aunt, but spent only a year in a first-grade classroom before following her heart to the acreage farmed by four generations of Finkmeyers.

"Simple people," one guest said, and rushed to add, "Simply marvelous."

"Gentle and generous."

A woman in blue lace delicately plucked a stuffed mushroom from the array. "Thank you, my dear," she murmured, not looking Gracie's way. "So unassuming! Yet his carvings! And he simply gave them to neighborhood ruffians!"

"The mirror here! In the nursery! Did you know he carved that? For his son, I believe —"

Gracie paused, attention riveted.

"The son who died? What was his name?"

"Will, I think. Or Bill — something like that."

"But they never went to church here, did they?"

"Long ago. That tiny chapel beyond Mason City was where they felt called. . . ."

"And no one bakes like Sadie! Give her a cup of flour and a teaspoon of vanilla —"

Gracie passed to another table. *Did You hear that, Lord? But what a silly thing to ask! You guided his knife while the ark took shape, and those delightful animals! But to lose a son, and then — rather than wrap the mirror away in some drawer for later spurts of grieving — to give joy to others. . . .*

Lost in thought, she nearly tipped the tray dangerously close to a balding head.

"Just in time!" the near-victim said. "How did you know I was on the verge of starvation?" Taking one of everything, he asked impishly, "Will you marry me?" And, shaking her head, Gracie continued on a wave of shared laughter.

"— nearly lost the farm in the Depression, I hear."

"Yet never accepted help. Not from family or neighbors — not that any had much of their own. And not from the government."

Returning to the kitchen with her empty tray, Gracie whispered, "I have to go somewhere. Just for a minute."

Marge nodded knowingly, and Gracie didn't correct her. It wasn't the bathroom she wanted, but the nursery — to see if the mirror had been restored to its rightful spot. Surely — before they left — the Finkmeyers would want to see Lorenzo's handiwork again.

Later, as the elderly couple endeavored to cut the cake — one of Gracie's triple layers, its columns adorned painstakingly with climbing vines and delicate red roses — Sadie dropped the knife. It landed point down on Lorenzo's polished right shoe. Gallantly, he forgave her with a hug. "Only the third time in sixty years she's thrown a knife at me."

"Renzie!" She jabbed him in the ribs with her elbow, then chuckled. "Actually, it's the fourth," and threw him a "take-that!" grin.

He hugged her close, cake and knife suddenly unimportant, and the crowd clapped and hooted approval.

In the kitchen, Marge looked up from a tray of crinkled paper cups holding scoops of ice cream. "I'm so envious! They were probably high school sweethearts." She sighed. "And I still vote for the inkwell!"

Uncle Miltie clattered trays into the sink. "Nope. I know for a fact."

So did Gracie, refilling a crystal plate of rose-shaped mints — but she wasn't about to say that they had met much later.

Marge waved a butter-pecan scoop in mid-air. When Uncle Miltie said no more, she finally snapped. *"Well?"*

He added enough soap powder for a bubble bath.

Gracie feared the ice cream might melt before the impasse resolved itself.

Marge's eyes blazed. "You are the most *infuriating —*"

Infuriating, but dear, Gracie thought. She said gently, "Uncle Miltie. . . ."

"His last name —" he clanked silverware into a metal strainer "— *begins with 'F'.*"

Marge thumped the scoop to the table, banging the edge of the tray. "What difference would it make if his name *was* Adam or Anthony? Or *Ziccardo,* for that matter!"

"Not much," Uncle Miltie said evenly — with effort, Gracie was certain — "except that then he *might* have dipped her pigtails in his inkwell." He turned, his eyes dancing, his fingertips dripping soapsuds. "Give up?"

From the reception room, laughter exploded. Someone picked out a one-fingered tune. "Don't Sit Under the Apple Tree."

Nodding grimly, Marge resumed arranging ice cream according to color.

"Teachers put students in alphabetical order then. Maybe they still do. Nobody that close to a teacher's desk would take the chance. Not to mention — only way she could've been in front of him was to have a name like Farrow or Fenton . . . or something."

Marge shrugged. "Then he was in World War Two," she said, shaping a new fantasy inspired by the music emanating from the

78

large room — "and wounded. She was the nurse who saved his life."

"Nope."

Marge stamped her foot. *"Nope?"* she shrieked.

"You didn't notice he limps?"

Marge slammed ice cream cups until the table shook. *"War wound!"*

"Nope." He washed and rinsed three plates before continuing. "Polio."

"That could have come later. The vaccine wasn't available until —"

"He was seven. Nearly died."

Marge said, "You're guessing!"

"Nope."

Gracie threw a chiding look Uncle Miltie ignored. For one thing, his back was turned, his shoulders shaking with laughter. "He was eavesdropping earlier, Marge, dear."

Drying his hands, he asked innocently, "Gracie, why don't I take these empty boxes to the van?"

The streamers were down, balloons and centerpieces taken, major leftovers boxed and sent home with the Finkmeyer grandchildren, tables folded and stored, floor vacuumed, dishes and utensils in their proper places. Everything was done except those final little details Gracie liked to take care of herself — alone. It was a winding-down time she always cherished.

Forgive me, Lord, for being selfish. But when I get home — much as You know I love them — both Gooseberry and Uncle Miltie will need me, and just now I want to relax. Stare into space. And bend Your ear a bit about that delightful couple, how You've blessed them with such an enduring love. Their teasing was so endearing. I think that must please You, too. But they're frail. One of these times — life being what it is — one may be left alone.

Tears smarted her eyes. *She* had been left alone — well, almost — and that had been difficult enough. But Sadie and Renzie Finkmeyer had become two parts of one whole — as inseparable as the warp and weft of a tapestry, or bark fused to the trunk of a sapling.

Her thoughts drifted, spiraling lazily like dust motes.

Those windows could stand a good cleaning. But not today, Lord. It's time I go —

Somewhere, a door opened. Stealthily? — or only slowly, tentatively, as though unsure of a welcome?

And which door had it been?

If Pastor Paul had driven over to secure the church, he'd have seen her car, and surely called a greeting.

80

Her ears strained for further creakings.

If the Finkmeyers had forgotten anything, they'd have come directly here. And no one else would feel the need to slink around, either.

Could it be the mysterious thief? If so, could there be anything to dread from someone who returned more than he took? It depended, she supposed, on how important secrecy was — and why it was necessary at all.

She glanced around for a hiding place. Was her heartbeat actually as loud as it sounded to her? She found herself holding her breath. This was silly! — she'd certainly been through escapades far more worthy of pulse-pounding!

Still, it was late evening and she was alone here.

Or — worse — *not* alone?

"Is there someone there?" she called, forbidding her voice to quaver.

At first, no answer. Only a vibrating silence, as though someone held his or her breath as Gracie's own stayed suspended.

And then a quick shuffle of footsteps and a cheery, "Ah! I've found you then!"

Even before she saw the figure, she recognized the voice.

"Pierre! Whatever —"

"Whatever, indeed!" he said. "I planned to get here in time to help, and they kept me busy with other things."

"To help —"

"With your party, of course! And now everyone's gone, and," he glanced around, "it's all cleaned up." His tongue flicked along his lower lip. "It is all cleaned up . . . ?"

"Cleaned up, but not completely gone." She had saved some broken peanut butter brownies to be crumbled over Uncle Miltie's ice cream before bedtime, with a few for herself and a mere taste for Gooseberry. And there might be some scoops of ice cream left in the freezer. "Only water to drink, I'm afraid."

"No lemon?"

She found a half, and he squeezed the juice into a glass. "When life hands you lemons," he said, and waved airily.

"You make lemonade," she finished.

"Or lemon pie . . . lemon soufflé . . . lemon and egg soup . . . chicken breasts with lemon and herbs. . . ." He shrugged. "But *un citron pressé* quite suffices!" He swished the juice in the glass. "Ice? Sugar? Though artificial sweetener would do — in the blue packet. They do it deliberately, you know. Not a bit subtly. Though I let them think they're putting it over on me, so when the time comes for my master plan —" He clamped his lips firmly, and made the zipping motion she had seen small children make when quietness was called for. "Ice?" he repeated. "Sugar?"

"Who are *'they'*?" she asked, complying with a casualness she didn't feel.

He hesitated while he measured the sugar carefully.

She imagined him judging how much he should confide.

Then, shrugging, he said matter-of-factly, "The *gendarmes*, of course. That's what we call them in Paris, where I studied as a young chef. *Paree*, that would be. *Gendarmes* sounds grander, more official, but it all adds up to restraint in the end, doesn't it?" He slid to the sink, and poured until the glass brimmed. "There's enough for two. . . ."

"No, thank you," she said.

"Good! Otherwise we'd be required to do the 'Half-full, half-empty' routine." He took a long sip. "Lovely! Better than red or white wine, yellow lemonade, especially with —" His eyes brightened. "The dessert tray?"

There were only a scoop of French vanilla — appropriate, she thought — and the brownie crumbs, so she supplemented with a saucer of ancient Ritz crackers she'd found in a drawer. Smiling, laying aside his now neon-pink cap, Pierre tugged the repast toward him, bowed his head briefly, and began.

Dear Lord . . . he said grace! He may not know a retirement home attendant from a gendarme *. . . but he remembers Whom to thank — even for brownie crumbs and stale Ritz crackers. . . .*

"*Magnifique!*" he was saying, rising from his chair. "I must have — I *demand!* — the recipe!"

"Of course," she began. She'd always been partial to that particular brownie herself.

But it was a Ritz cracker that he held, that he regarded with awe — that he lifted in an ecstatic salute.

They were just approaching Fannie Mae, Gracie's venerable Cadillac, when Pastor Paul arrived to secure the church for the evening. "Climb in, Pierre," he invited. "I'll drive you home. Gracie, why don't you join us for the ride? I'll bring you back to your car."

Pierre seemed happy enough to return to Pleasant Haven. Scrambling from the backseat — where he had insisted he sit alone for the protection of his Ritz cracker — he waved jauntily and sprinted off toward one of the residence buildings.

Gracie watched him go while Paul, smiling, began backing from their parking spot.

"Paul! Oh, Paul!" The voice was light and musical. Even without looking, Gracie knew that it was Blaise Bloomfield.

Ahhhh, she thought, and turned to see the lovely young woman gesturing frantically as she hurried in and out of shadows unreached by the tall parking lot lights. Flushed and out of breath, she leaned on the driver's side of the car. She was too young, Gracie knew, her physical condition obviously too good, for the color and breathlessness to result only from that slight exertion.

Blaise placed her ringless left hand on Paul's, as it rested on the steering wheel.

He didn't move it, Gracie noticed.

"Mrs. Parks." Blaise leaned into the car slightly. "I just wanted to check, really — to be sure things are advancing smoothly for our gathering — to ask if there's any way I can help."

"You're very kind." Gracie tried to keep her smile from spreading too broadly. "I'll let you know if there is."

"I was afraid I might not see you in church Sunday." She patted Pastor Paul's hand. "You will be picking . . . some of us up in the morning?"

"I plan to," he said. "At least someone will."

"I do hope it's you!" She added hastily, "Otherwise, Mrs. McAdoo would be deeply dismayed."

And Mrs. McAdoo would not be alone in her disappointment, Gracie thought.

"Good-bye, then!" Giving his hand a final squeeze, Blaise stepped back and away.

Gracie supposed she looked like Alice's Cheshire cat, sitting there, grinning in the near dark. Fortunately, Pastor Paul paid strict attention to his driving as they completed the turn and started down the driveway.

"Is there a chance, do you think," he asked after they had driven in silence for a few blocks, "is there any chance Pierre's the one doing these swaps?"

Obviously, Blaise Bloomfield would not be a topic of conversation. Did that mean that he wanted to keep the voice, the touches, the budding intimacy to himself, to think more about when he was alone? Or did it simply mean he had dismissed them as inconsequential?

He gave no clue, simply asked again, "Could he be, do you think?"

Gracie considered. Pierre had stamina enough for the walk, obviously. He was persistent — unquestionably. And if the "swaps" had involved kitchen implements — or more particularly, recipe books — she'd have no doubt. But what would Pierre, with his cooking fixation, want with carved mirrors or offering plates? Where would he have found a Beatrix Potter print? Would he have the interest or capability of writing poetic riddles?

"It sounds more like Uncle Miltie than Pierre," she said casually, then drew a sharp breath.

Pastor Paul slowed for a road sign. "I hadn't wanted to suggest that. . . ."

"But he'd come to mind?"

She could hear the smile in his voice. "Whenever there's mischief abroad, Uncle Miltie comes to mind *first!*"

It was true, of course. Uncle Miltie was irrepressible. That refusal to grow stodgy and serious was a large part of his charm. But. . . .

"I remember another time I suspected him —" Then it had been a potato salad that tasted weirdly like bananas, and he'd been deeply hurt at her suggestion. "If he were going to do something like this — why wait until now?"

"You've been so busy —"

"Neglecting him?" Had she? Thinking

back, she could remember many times when he'd patted the cushion of her favorite rocker and invited her to watch TV with him. "But I've *always* been busy. . . ."

Gooseberry, as well, had voiced displeasure at the recent lack of attention paid to him. "Arlen was like that," she mused, "when he was a child." Once he had hidden all her spices — come to think of it, he'd turned the whole thing into a treasure hunt. "It can't be," she said on a long-drawn sigh. Might Arlen have told Uncle Miltie of his escapade? "What now?"

"There's no real harm been done."

"Yet?"

"Yet," he agreed. "Look, Gracie, why don't I invite him to go fishing Monday, while you do . . . whatever you need to do."

"But that's your only day off! Your day to —"

"— go fishing," he finished. "And can you imagine anything more deadly than sitting in a rowboat going nowhere . . . with no one to share the experience but the inhabitants of the bait can?"

What a sweet young man he is, Lord, she thought as he brought her back to the parking lot and her own car. *A true shepherd of Your sheep. How blessed we are to have him here at Eternal Hope — a constant reminder of*

Your love. And if he and this young woman should be in Your plan. . . . But then, that's none of my business, is it, Lord?

Paul leaned across, opening the passenger door. "Fannie Mae awaits," he said.

"How can I thank you?" she asked.

"Brownies would be nice." He laughed. "Now you get on home and sit on that rocking chair. Watch TV and eat popcorn. You hear?"

She heard. And the prospect sounded more than inviting. She wondered, however, if any of the programs on television that night could possibly be as enticing as the unanswered questions in Willow Bend's real life. And that included the possibly budding relationship between Pastor Paul and Blaise Bloomfield.

5

Lacey was hanging limply over the tire swing when Gracie approached Fountain's Tourist Home. Even Gooseberry expressed alarm — until the child looked up, struggled from her unnatural posture and came screeching to meet them.

The swing on the porch was occupied by a couple who were evidently newlyweds. The rest of the world might have evaporated, Gracie noted with a reminiscent smile, for all their apparent awareness.

How well she remembered. . . .

But Lacey alternately bounced and lavished affection on Gooseberry, each of them managing to look expectant.

Cookies.

Ah, yes.

Gracie fished a small plastic bag from one cavernous pocket of her exercise suit. "Peanut butter," she explained, then erased Lacey's frown with, "and I used some chunks of milk chocolate, just for color."

"I love color!" Lacey purred, and tore into

the treat. Gooseberry watched with unconcealed interest.

"Lace!" a harsh voice called from an upper window of the historic house, which had once been a haven for runaway slaves, as Cordelia was fond of pointing out. "In here, *now!*"

The newlyweds took no note.

Another face, this time a man's, appeared beside and slightly behind the apparently frazzled Aunt Kelly.

"It's all his fault," Lacey muttered. "I *hate* Uncle Grif!"

Gracie sighed.

Gooseberry's pleased purr dipped to sadness, but whether it was because of Lacey's need or his own failure to beg a peanut butter crumb, Gracie wasn't certain.

Lord, hatred should have no place in this sweet child's heart. Please erase its poison and replace her frown with gladness. . . .

"I have to go, or they'll —" Lacey hugged the bag of cookies.

"They're for you, dear."

"Lacey!" Aunt Kelly's summons was shrill.

Pausing in flight, Lacey pleaded, "Will you come back?"

"When we've finished our walk."

The child's face brightened, Gooseberry

growled deep in his furry orange throat. And the honeymooners merely adjusted their clinch.

Gracie had gone less than a mile — Gooseberry's meanderings might have been greater — when a silver late-model sports car scooted past and braked with a squeal.

Gracie noticed first the cloud of pale blue hair.

Eudora McAdoo. Amazing! The hair tone seemed to have altered slightly just since church!

"I've been looking for you!" Eudora trilled. Leaving the car where it was, she carefully checked all doors to be certain they were locked — even though side windows gaped open. "We can't be too careful, can we?" she asked, "with all that's going on." Her jogging suit gave off a high-tech metallic shine, its colors pale blue and silver.

To match her hair and her car? Gracie wondered. The woman took coordination to dizzying new dimensions!

"You don't mind if I walk with you? And chat about next Saturday's gala? I'm delighted that you've asked the choir to do a few numbers! My dear, is it necessary that we do the hundred-yard dash?"

With her beringed hand, she caught

Gracie's wrist. Sunlight ignited an assortment of diamonds, rendering Gracie temporarily blind. "I'm completely out of breath already!" And Eudora collapsed against a faded picket fence as though to prove it.

Gracie paused, waiting, and blinking against spots. Gooseberry, less patient, followed some invisible trail only he could see into roadside weeds. *At least that's what he wants us to believe,* Gracie thought. In all likelihood, he planned to lurk somewhere in comparative peace until Hurricane Eudora had spent herself.

Actually, as they strolled along, Gracie found herself enjoying the experience. True, she'd have gotten more exercise sitting at her kitchen table working a crossword puzzle. And, doubly true, she missed her habitual talk with God; she'd have to do that later. But the woman was well worth getting to know.

"I don't plan to live at Pleasant Haven forever," she confided. "My late husband and I traveled the world. We made safaris, walked the Great Wall. I went snorkeling beyond coral reefs, even hacked through a jungle or two." She sighed, slowing down even more, something Gracie would have thought impossible while still maintaining movement.

"I'd always expected he'd die from shark-bite or black mamba venom or something equally exotic. Somehow, choking to death on a barbecued beef sandwich never presented itself as a possibility."

"I'm so sorry," Gracie murmured, wondering why such an ignominious dying should seem any less a loss.

"I miss him terribly."

Gracie nodded, understanding fully. Never a day passed but she yearned to share some concern or pleasure or bit of news with El.

"But then," Eudora brightened, "life must go on! There's a gentleman at Pleasant Haven I talk with often — he came to church with us, that Sunday after your choir's performance. Uses oxygen, you may remember. His adventures are entertaining, though not nearly as amusing as others I've heard — and his details are never the same twice in a row. He'll be speaking of Grenada, and all of a sudden, he's trekking across Antarctica, or somewhere. You may have met him?" Not waiting for a response, she continued, "I myself am quite ready — for whatever adventure may lie ahead! I've never been to Cleveland."

Cleveland? Gracie gulped. Someone who had walked the Great Wall of China, who had embraced the possibility of ravenous sharks and raging lions, wanted to visit Cleveland?

"Whatever for?" she couldn't help asking.

Shrugging, Eudora said, "New worlds to conquer, I suppose." She smiled dreamily, then shook herself, asking, "Well, have you rested long enough? I'm eager to move on!"

During the ensuing snail's-paced mile, Gracie learned that as a young person Eudora had worked in fragrances in a department store ("quite a huge department, actually, the backbone of the total first floor") that she had visited the Mayan ruins ("what marvelous flora and fauna — well actually I avoided as much of the fauna as possible — and some of the flora could also be, I suppose, quite detrimental to one's health") and had always ached for children. However, she and her husband had been, for unknown reasons, denied that particular blessing. "And you?"

"A son," Gracie said. "Arlen." The joy of their lives, hers and El's, though she wouldn't voice anything to add to Eudora's sense of deprivation.

"Perhaps God knew what He was doing."

Gracie smiled. "Doesn't He always?"

"Usually, I suspect." Eudora seemed quite sincere in limiting God's scope. "In the case of children. . . ." Her voice faded — but not for long.

Gracie suspected that there might not be an off switch wired into Eudora's circuitry.

"However could we have traipsed around the world with a child in tow? No, much better for us that we were unencumbered."

And certainly better for any child! Gracie was already entertaining some reservations about Eudora and her level of self-absorption. *Forgive me, Lord. It isn't up to me to judge —*

She was glad she hadn't voiced her thoughts aloud when Eudora continued quietly, "Still, I would have foregone every adventure we enjoyed to have the pleasure of children about me!" She stooped to caress the petals of a hollyhock. "I must be getting back. I believe I parked my car somewhat askew. Do come visit me!" she invited. "Oh, and bring that delightful older brother with you."

Older brother? Gracie frowned. She must mean —

"The man who tells such wonderful jokes."

"Uncle Miltie. Well, yes, he does tell jokes." To Gracie's knowledge, no one ever before had applied the adjective *wonderful* to George Morgan. Except maybe Aunt Dora.

"Your uncle! How jolly your home must be — that is, if he's always so humorous?"

"Nearly always, yes."

"Or I could come visit you — wherever you live."

Gracie, thinking how her work might suffer in such conversational onslaught, said, "I'm certain we'll sing at Pleasant Haven whenever Pastor Paul wants us."

Eudora's expression screwed into an attitude of contemplation. "I've been thinking I might audition for your church choir."

"That would be nice. Especially if you're an alto."

"I could be, I suppose."

"I was joking, really. It's just that the alto section gets lonely, at times."

"I sang high soprano in school. Solos, even." She smiled, adding, "My husband said he fell in love with my high C before he noticed me."

Competition for the high notes might be good for Estelle, Gracie thought, not without humor. Though it would be disastrous, of course, for maintaining any semblance of balance in the choir. Briefly, she pictured the congregation cringing while mezzo-sopranos dueled to some laryngitic resolution.

"Well, dear." Eudora placed her diamond-studded hand on Gracie's arm. "I can't tell you how I've enjoyed our talk! How I look forward to visiting with you again! And, of course, with your uncle. 'Bye now!" And she set off at a clip Gracie would have been hard put to emulate.

"Well, Gooseberry," she said moments later when the feline deigned to make his eminent presence known. "What do you make of that?"

Gooseberry's silence was answer enough.

Lord, she never did say why she'd been looking for me, did she? Gracie searched back through their conversation — if such a monologue qualified for the term. Was it to test whether or not she'd be welcomed by the choir? Is she simply lonely — and sensed sisterhood in someone who also helps her hair color along a bit? Unconsciously, Gracie fluffed her hair. It was getting a bit shaggy — she'd need to make an appointment once her schedule eased. . . . *Did You send her? Was there something You would have had me say — given the chance? What am I missing here?*

And the thought came suddenly with such clarity that she repeated it aloud. "She's interested in Uncle Miltie! Romantically!"

Gooseberry peered up at the sound of her voice, then twined himself, purring, around her ankles.

She paused to rub the soft warm fur between his ears. *Is that it, Lord?*

It should have been obvious! Eudora's hanging on Uncle Miltie's every word that first day, when Blaise Bloomfield had urged choir and residents to "mingle." Her preening and simpering — yes, those were appropriate words — after church. In a way, it was rather charming, two over-the-hill teenagers having a crush. Or, at least there was a crush coming from one direction on a collision course! But how Gracie would miss Uncle Miltie if he decided to take another wife and make a new life for himself!

But I guess I'm getting ahead of myself, right, Lord? I have a tendency to do that sometimes. As You well know.

Aunt Kelly and her darkly glowering husband sat on the tourist home porch, sipping drinks from tall frosted glasses, while a dispirited Lacey plucked blades of grass and chucked them toward a spider web arcing between two rhododendron bushes.

Gooseberry ran to Lacey — instantly restoring the child's energy and sparkle — while Gracie approached the adults on the porch. "Good afternoon," she said brightly.

There was no answer. The couple barely acknowledged her presence.

"Would it be all right, I wonder, if I took Lacey to visit her grandmother?"

"Oh, yes, yes, yes, yes, *yes!*" Lacey pleaded. She raised her hands prayerfully. "Please, please, *please,* Aunt Kelly!"

To Gracie, it seemed a simple request, but apparently not to the couple on the porch. Frowning, Kelly looked to her husband, and he studied the idea carefully, turning his glass at least five full revolutions before saying roughly, "We were just thinking of going ourselves."

"But I want to go with *Goose*berry!" Lacey's foot stopped just short of a stomp.

Kelly sighed.

She looks so tired, Lord. Help me to be softer in my judgment. It's difficult having a mother who's so ill, and then taking on the care of a child. Not to mention living under a strange roof in a strange town, all the while forced to bow to the decisions of a domineering husband.

"Grif, would it really hurt —"

He shot her a warning look.

Kelly didn't make eye contact. "We'll take her," she said. "But you and the cat could meet her there."

Grif didn't seem too happy about that, either.

★ ★ ★

Lacey waited, alone, by the arbor. "Aunt Kelly and Uncle Grif didn't want me to go with them. They said they'd bring Gram here and I could wait for you." She frowned. "Uncle Grif tried to be nice — and it always scares me when that happens." She brightened. "You *did* bring Gooseberry!"

The two entangled in a giggling, purring embrace.

Gracie settled at one end of a stone bench that managed to be cold even though the thermometer had set records for the date. "How do you mean, scares you?" she asked, once Lacey and Gooseberry were content to sit beside her. A thousand terrible possibilities flashed through her mind.

Lacey screwed up her face. "Not *scares*, exactly. Just makes me wonder — what he's thinking." She leaned closer and whispered conspiratorially. "Gram never trusted Uncle Grif. Once she found him and Aunt Kelly going through her bank stuff. She said she'd shot lots of possums in the henhouse in her day, and she could always shoot another."

Her voice grew a bit pensive as she added, "I always thought baby possums were cute . . . and even the mothers, with their pink noses and fuzzy fur, if their tails didn't look like rat tails. It bothered me, Gram shooting them, or anything."

"I think possums steal eggs," Gracie comforted. "I'm sure your grandmother shot them only because she had to."

Lacey's legs swung briskly. "And even though she didn't say anything about the bank stuff, Aunt Kelly put it away awful fast, and old Uncle Grif said he'd better get back to Chicago 'cause he had a 'pointment. I thought that was funny — just because of some possums. Then Uncle Grif growled at Aunt Kelly, 'You comin' or not?' and Gram said, real firm, '*Not!* My *daughter's* staying for dinner.' But we didn't have dinner 'til real late that night. Gram and Aunt Kelly were in Gram's bedroom, and I heard somebody cryin'."

She hugged Gooseberry so tightly he struggled to be free and plopped to the pavement, doing figure-eights around Gracie's ankles. He tried with Lacey's, but her feet were too far off the ground.

"And then, not long after, Gram *fell*. At least that's what *they* say." The child's lips trembled, then grew rigid.

Gracie knew that she should somehow stem the flood of confidences. But surely it helped Lacey to have a chance to talk these things out with someone who'd listen. And it would help Gracie reach the child, the more she knew about her situation. *Or am I just being nosy, Lord?* She squirmed on the seat. "It sounds to me," she said, "as though your Aunt Kelly is very unhappy."

Lacey nodded. "When Uncle Grif stays away for a lot of days, she seems happier. And nicer, too. I told her that one day, but she just glared and told me I had horrendous manners. And that was the last time she was nice to me all that day."

She sighed. "I *want* to love her. Mama did." Another sigh. "But then Mama loved everyone."

"*There* you are!"

Gracie would never have recognized the voice as Grif Ransen's. She turned to be certain. His mouth curved to show white teeth — and although it was shaped like a smile, above it his eyes were hard, and cold. And calculating. *Or am I reading too much into this, Lord? Is this an opportunist, capable of who-knows-what deviltry? Or is he the caring son-in-law he appears to be now, gently guiding a sick woman's wheelchair over the pathway into cooling shade?*

And what of Kelly, silent as she walked stiffly beside her husband, her glance hooded? She kept one hand on his arm, as though her own movement originated through his muscles. Once, when she bent to shake a pebble from her shoe, he turned his sharp glance on her, and she mumbled what seemed to be an apology.

Gooseberry meowed a question, then opted to return to the bench, as Gracie and Lacey followed her relatives down the path toward aspen shadow.

Once the wheelchair was settled and an afghan draped over Gillian Pomeroy's lap, Lacey approached delicately, almost on tiptoe, her arms reaching out. "Gram," she said softly, dropping to her knees.

Swallowing around a lump in her throat, Gracie dabbed at the corners of her eyes.

Slowly, ever so slowly, Gram's hands lifted.

"Oh, Gram!" Lacey hugged the unresponsive, sagging shoulders.

Yet not quite unresponsive! The trembling hands moved again, catching Lacey's back and tugging her even closer. For a moment they clutched there, then dropped away.

Lacey turned a face streaming with tears. "Gracie? Did *God* do that?"

"I wouldn't be surprised," Gracie whispered, just as Grif snorted and Gram's lips moved. Lacey, dabbing her eyes, seemed not to notice, but Gracie watched and listened intently.

"Dr-r-rug-g —" The woman licked her lips, moving them together, then tried again. "Dr-r-r —"

It had been barely a whisper, but there was no question what the woman had said, although the meaning was certainly open to interpretation.

Gracie felt a hand on her shoulder, moving her to one side. "There, there, Mother Pomeroy." Grif positioned himself so that Gram's face was hidden from everyone else.

At the same time, Gracie thought grimly, everyone else also was hidden from Gram.

"Kelly," he commanded, and Aunt Kelly moved beside him. Between the two of them, they formed an impenetrable barrier.

"Lacey," Kelly said over her shoulder, "take your friend to the parking lot or somewhere. We shouldn't have brought Mom outside, so close to the time for her medication." Glaring at Gracie, she said, "You heard her asking for it!" Then she turned her back.

Lacey stood, hands fisted at her sides, tears once more streaming down her cheeks.

"Come," Gracie urged gently. There seemed no use in their doing anything other than obey.

At least for now.

Gooseberry joined them when they had

resumed their places on the stone bench near the main entrance of Gram's building. "They always do that," Lacey muttered. "They don't let me go with them when they bring her out, and then — whenever she shows any sign that she hears me — they send me away." She raised tear-filled eyes. "That day you found us, you and that pretty Amy? They didn't know I'd come. Well, not at first, anyway. A nurse helped me get her wheelchair out, and said she'd be back later. But I bet you remember Uncle Grif watching! If Gram had moved or tried to talk, you can bet he'd have been there, pushing me away again!"

Gracie felt a pleasant chill — an idea. Not, perhaps, what Pastor Paul would approve, let alone God, but she'd talk to at least one of them about it.

"What if you and I came sometime . . . without their knowing?"

Lacey caught both Gracie's hands and bounced. Gooseberry instantly sought sanctuary beneath the bench. "Yes! Oh, let's! Only . . ." Her smile faded. "Now Aunt Kelly always makes me promise to stay in the yard at Miss Cordelia's when she's gonna be gone for long. And I wouldn't mind breaking my promise, but you —" She shrugged.

The child was right, of course. Gracie

couldn't encourage going directly against a guardian's orders. *But there must be a way around this, Lord, isn't there? If You could defeat the Midianites with lamps and pitchers — tricking them into thinking they were being attacked by hordes? And, besides, didn't you say we should be wily as serpents?*

"How would it be," she asked, choosing to neglect the other portion of the serpent reference, the part about being innocent as doves, "if I'd invite you for a day of baking cookies? We'd have to choose our recipes, then shop for ingredients."

"And there's a grocery store really close!" No trace of sadness remained in the child's eyes. Gracie loved the resilience of the young, the way moods lifted like the changing of channels.

"And it would be unconscionable to be so close, and not —"

"Drop by to visit Gram!" Lacey finished ecstatically, then leaned closer, peered from beneath her eyelids and said in pseudo-seriousness, "Oh, my, yes, dear Mrs. Parks! Unconsh— Unconsh—able, indeed!"

They both turned at the sound of the whir of wheels. Gram, now sagging once more, was being wheeled back to the building.

"God isn't doing very well, is He?"

Gracie started.

"With my prayer. Maybe it's all just a big waste of time —"

Gracie's hand closed over Lacey's. "Never!" she insisted. "Prayer is never, ever a waste of time!"

"Well —" Lacey shrugged away. "He's sure working awful slow, if He's working at all."

But Gracie was fairly certain that — in this case — God might welcome some human help.

6

Lord, what was I thinking? Gracie slit open five packets of dry yeast and emptied them into separate bowls, then measured and added warm water. Milk was nearly scalded on her front burner, eggs already warming to room temperature on the counter. *How could I have rashly promised the child anything when I need this whole week for baking and cooking?*

She'd totally forgotten during that moment with Lacey how hectic her week would be, preparing for Pleasant Haven's Family Day.

"Plan for at least one hundred fifty," Blaise Bloomfield had instructed her.

This morning, it seemed, *everything* was a problem! Marge had called to say mournfully that her beloved Charlotte was listless and possibly had a fever. That meant she had to run the dog to the vet before racing off to her shop to unpack a special shipment. "But I can be with you tomorrow, Gracie," she'd promised brightly. "At least I *think* I can. At least part of the day."

Gracie had been counting heavily on Marge. *I should know better, Lord*, she admitted. *Marge is . . . well, Marge is* Marge. *Not that she's irresponsible on purpose. Actually, not that she's irresponsible at all — just terminally flaky.* Gracie smiled. *Which is why we're friends, I suppose. But please, Lord, help Lacey to forget my promise until after this impossible week!*

She paused, her measuring cup overflowing with flour. Flushing, she felt guilty of insufferable self-centeredness. *And please, about Charlotte? And Marge's own business demands? Please help Marge through her day . . . and be with everyone else You can think of, but I don't have time to. But especially Lacey — if she could just be content at Cordelia's, at least for the next few days.*

As if in direct rebuttal, a light tap on the door preceded Lacey's light call, "I'm here, Gracie! Aunt Kelly said I could come to bake cookies! And Uncle Grif just grunted, so I figured that meant 'okay'."

Gracie dreaded what the child would surely ask next — how soon they could visit her grandmother. Instead, heaving a gigantic sigh, but seeming cheerful enough, she settled onto a high stool and finished, "it was Uncle Grif, though, who remembered to say if I went anywhere but right here and back, he'd find out and make me sorry."

"Dear child —"

"I just wish," Lacey told her, "that he knew how sorry I am even to know him! And ac-shully, Gracie — how sorry I am for Aunt Kelly." She confided, "I didn't really know that until just now. Isn't it funny how — when you talk stuff out, even to yourself — you see things clearer?"

Carefully, Gracie measured vanilla. "I find that when I talk to God."

The stool nearly toppled. "You talk to God? I mean, you really, ac-shully, honest and truly *talk* to Him?"

Gracie smiled. "I was 'really, actually, honest and truly' talking to Him just before you knocked." Oops. What if Lacey asked exactly what she'd been saying? To forestall the possibility, Gracie continued, "I was praying about many of my friends — including you."

"Me?" Lacey's hands clasped over her narrow chest. "Oh, Gracie, I don't think anyone ever prayed about *me!*" She sobered, remembering. "Gram did. Oh, *Gracie —*"

"I know, child. I know." Had it not been for her floury hands and apron, she would have hugged Lacey. Surely the best thing was to keep her occupied. "Now how would

111

you like to help me? I'm afraid we may not have time today for cookies."

"I don't care! What do I do?" She was off the stool and ready for duty. Gracie wouldn't have been surprised at a sharp salute.

"Wash your hands first. Really well! With soap!" she added, remembering Arlen at Lacey's age, though girls might be different. "And you'll find an apron on the back of that chair."

By the time Uncle Miltie and Gooseberry came in from napping in the hammock, Gracie had the various doughs rising, and Lacey was busy at a cutting board, chopping nuts.

Uncle Miltie frowned, "It's faster to —" but he stopped at Gracie's warning glance. She certainly didn't want Lacey handling anything with vicious blades and/or requiring electricity. "What do you have for me to do, Gracie?"

"I need some apples cored and sliced."

"Not pared?"

"They're Granny Smiths." Whenever possible, she liked to leave the peelings on. Why put the best nutrients and color in the garbage?

Gooseberry meowed from the doorway. He knew full well that the kitchen was out-of-bounds when a catering job loomed.

"Just go relax," she told her cat, and he stalked off, almost certainly affronted.

"He misses Charlotte," Uncle Miltie said from the sink, where he washed his hands — with soap. "Marge tell you she had to leave her at the vet's? Just a cold, I guess, but Doc Wilkins wanted to be sure." Uncle Miltie raised his voice over the splashing of water across a colander heaped with apples. "I've been watching Gooseberry for any symptoms."

Lacey asked worriedly, "Gooseberry is okay then, huh?" Her small paring knife hung over a small mountain of walnuts.

"He is A-OK, honey." Uncle Miltie turned, eyes twinkling. "Got a question maybe you could answer. Do you know the difference between a circus lion and an animal cracker?"

Lacey giggled. "Everybody does!"

"Then tell me."

Lacey's face screwed up thoughtfully. "Well, one roars and one doesn't."

"Try again."

"One has fur and one doesn't?"

"Again?"

"One's alive and one isn't!"

"True. But, again?"

"One's made up of meat and one's a cookie?" The child was looking as frustrated

113

as Gracie always felt when faced with one of Uncle Miltie's clunky puzzlers. In the meantime, no nuts were getting chopped — and no apples quartered.

Uncle Miltie must have caught his niece's expression, for he said, "You bite the head off an animal cracker, but the circus lion bites the head off you!"

"Ha, ha!" Lacey whooped. "That's a really, really good one! Isn't it, Gracie?"

Gracie only smiled, shaking her head.

Now, maybe they'd get some work done.

As the morning wore on, they worked quietly. When the mixer wasn't in use, there were only the tick of the oven-timer, the swish of water in the sink, the crunching of nut meats and Gooseberry's snores.

"Would you like music?" Gracie asked when it was less than an hour until lunch time. It came as a surprise that her voice was rusty from lack of use.

"Uh huh," Lacey murmured.

Uncle Miltie, wearing an apron with a lobster dominating its front, looked up from mixing cinnamon and sugar. "Ever hear of child-labor laws, Gracie?" He nodded toward Lacey, leaning back to work her shoulders.

Gracie hadn't even noticed how weary the

child was becoming. "I think we have enough nuts for now. Why don't you go keep Gooseberry company until I get some lunch ready?"

"Honest, I'm not tired." She yawned, contradicting herself, then giggled. "Well, maybe a little." She inched out of her chair. "Could I take him a treat?"

Gracie indicated a plastic container of iced oatmeal cookies. "Take a few for yourself, too."

Lacey's hand poised above the container. "How many will Gooseberry want?"

"Rather, how many is Gooseberry allowed to have! Two at the most."

"Then I'll only take two for me, too."

Gracie and Uncle Miltie continued to work. Gracie rolled out dough so elastic it kept shrinking behind the rolling pin; Uncle Miltie spread a thin layer of the cinnamon-sugar mixture, then arranged sliced apples and walnuts, while Gracie carefully rolled everything into a long cylindrical shape, to be cut in slices, arranged in circular pans, and set to rise again.

She'd forgotten the music until — softly, at first — Lacey's thrilling voice began a lullabye. "Hush, little kitty, don't say a word . . . Lacey's gonna buy you —" She broke off. "Not a mockingbird!" she declared.

"You'd eat it! What else rhymes with *word?*"

Uncle Miltie, hearing her, called out possible answers. "Curd," he began, "furred, gird, herd, nerd, stirred —"

"I changed my mind," she said, "but thanks," and her voice resumed, "Hush, little kitty, don't say 'Meow,' Lacey's gonna buy you a milking cow." She called, "Gram told me once how *her* father used to spray milk into the kittens' mouths when he was milking!"

Gracie smiled, and Uncle Miltie chortled, "I've done that myself, a time or two!"

"If that milking cow won't . . . milk, Lacey's gonna dress you all up in silk!"

"Gooseberry'd have a thing or two to say about that!" Uncle Miltie glanced at the clock. "What have you planned for lunch, Gracie?"

"I haven't really planned anything . . . but would ham salad sandwiches fill the corners? With some corn chips?"

"Admirably!"

"If that silk gets ripped and old, Lacey's gonna get you . . . silver and gold!"

"Speaking of admirable," Uncle Miltie said gently, "have you ever in your life heard a voice like that?"

"Not in anyone so young! And seldom in anyone, no matter the age."

"And Estelle brags on her 'professional training.' " He shook his head. "Who could make her see the truth of it? That when it comes to nightingales, she's an old crow!"

His niece laughed as she cleared the last of the baking clutter from half of the table. "Would you get three of those plastic placemats, Uncle Miltie? And what would you think about my asking her to join the Eternal Hope choir?"

After lunch Gracie sat in the living room — eyes closed, feet propped on the ottoman, a copy of *Guideposts* lying open on her lap and the fragrances of baking apple, melting chocolate, rising dough and warm cat shaping a familiar bouquet all about her. Next to her, Gooseberry cocked an eyelid, then closed it.

Better than air freshener, Lord, she thought contentedly, *these scents which shape my world. Who could ask for more? I thank You for those I love and work I love, and for memories that show how I came to be here and for promises that allow me to face the future with expectation rather than dread.*

She hadn't meant to drift off, but when Gooseberry nudged her to wakefulness, she saw that the clock had advanced by half an hour, not the ten minutes she could have spared. Worse, her nose told her that if something wasn't burning, it was coming too close for comfort.

Gooseberry scrambled to a safe position while she hurried to salvage whatever might be in danger.

In the kitchen doorway, she stopped, unbelieving. The table was arranged with assorted goodies — some still steaming, all on racks or hot-pads, none burned. From one oven door, which stood ajar, tendrils of smoke rose from a small bubbling black mass beneath the bottom rack.

Something had boiled over. That was all. And Uncle Miltie and Lacey had things under total control.

"Gracie!" Lacey drew her closer to the oven. "Doesn't it look just like a volcano? A little one?"

Gracie had to agree. And Lacey herself looked like the aftermath of a whirlwind. Her hair was frizzed and her face sweat-streaked — with a smudge of what was obviously cinnamon across her nose — and one forefinger sported an angry burn.

Lacey extended it. "Your uncle ran cold water over it, and gave me some of that plant juice."

"Aloe," Gracie said. "Good for Uncle Miltie! But I'm afraid your Aunt Kelly won't let you visit again, if you go home looking as though you need an emergency room."

Lacey dismissed her aunt with a grimace. "*Gram* wouldn't mind. *Gram* would be happy! In fact, she'd be right here with us, doing stuff." Her sigh seemed to come from her toes. "And she will, won't she? Soon? God won't let us down, will He?"

The phone chose that moment to ring.

It was Barb, her voice shrill with agitation, calling from the daylong conference of regional choir directors she was attending. "Gracie, I can't believe the dumb thing I've done! — or, rather, haven't. That latest arrangement? The one I was going to bring with me? I think I may have put it in the piano bench. Or tucked it into the looseleaf hymnal, on the piano. Oh, dear, I hope I didn't take it home with me! You'd never find it there! But I wonder — could you possibly dash over to the church and fax it to me? The fax number's on the bulletin board. I tacked up an extra brochure. At least, I'm almost sure I did."

Just as Gracie pulled Fannie Mae in front of the church, Paul Meyer walked from the parking lot. He waited as she hurried up the sidewalk.

119

"Emergency?" he asked, smiling.

"Always!" She paused for a deep breath. "Not mine, this time, though."

"Barb's?"

"I'm impressed! How did you know?"

"She called me, too."

Gracie shook her head. "I wonder how many others —"

"She was afraid you wouldn't know how to use the fax." He held the door for her. "So how's the catering coming?"

"Well, fine, I suppose, but it didn't help that Marge had some emergency at the store."

"The day for them, it seems. Would a clumsy minister be of any help in your kitchen?"

She wanted to hug him for being so thoughtful. "Actually, Uncle Miltie's helping —"

"Ah. Then perhaps —"

"And Lacey Carpenter."

He frowned.

"She hasn't been to church, but Uncle Miltie and I are thinking of asking her to join the choir. She's a real songstress, even at her age."

They stopped just within the sanctuary door.

"Again?" Pastor Paul sighed.

The offering plate was back — propped against the lectern, where it couldn't be missed. A poster board was braced behind it.

WHAT IS TALL, BUT FOLDS
    MUCH SMALLER . . .
STANDS ON THREE LEGS,
    "ARMS" OUT STRAIGHT?
RANSOM IT AND THEN RETURN
    IT, OR OUR CHOIR MIGHT BE
    IRATE.

SCARCELY NOTICED FOR ITS
    FUNCTION —
HELPING NOTES TO FALL AND
    RISE. . . .
EVEN THIEVES SHOULD HAVE
    COMPUNCTION
WHEN THE MUSIC . . .

D
I
E
S!

RANSOM: A REPRISE OF LAST
    WEEK'S WONDERFUL ANTHEM.

"The music stand?" What else *could* it be? "But why would anyone want to take that battered old thing?" Or presume we'd want it back, Gracie added in her thoughts as she hurried up the aisle, except possibly for Les Twomley, who would lose an important topic of conversation. She checked where it normally stood. Just as she'd thought — the metal stand was missing.

But something else was there.

"There's another clue," she said, and read it aloud:

IN THE MEANTIME, FOR YOUR
    PURPOSE,
USE A "LOANER," HIDDEN WELL.
MIGHT IT BE IN SOME FAR
    CLOSET?
LOOK AND FIND — FOR I WON'T
    TELL!

"One thing is certain," Gracie said from within the depths of the kitchen pantry, while Pastor Paul checked the broom closet and various other possibilities, "Uncle Miltie isn't the culprit."

"How can you be so sure?" Pastor Paul's voice was muffled, as though he spoke through thick fog.

"He'd never use the word *reprise*. He'd *know* it from crossword puzzles, or even from Scrabble, but he wouldn't use it, trust me."

"Gracie —" Pastor Paul emerged slowly, backwards, a cobweb caught in his hair.

"We're overdue for a cleaning day —" She broke off as he tugged a bulky wrapped item after him. Narrow in the long central section, the package broadened substantially at both ends.

"It's heavy," he said, "and the tag reads 'CHOIR.' Was Barb expecting anything?"

"Not that she mentioned."

He set it straight and stepped back. "Would you like to do the honors?"

She certainly would, but — "You do it," she said. "You found it, and you're the boss here."

"Since when?" he chuckled, but ripped at the top wrappings.

First came a glint of polished brass, then a gleaming, slanted surface, perhaps a foot in height and sixteen or eighteen inches in width — ornate with cutout S shapes and other curlicues.

"A . . . lectern?" he guessed.

But no, Gracie knew, even before he revealed the wide-stanced base, each foot ending in a spiral. It was a music stand. She had seen one like this only twice, first in the window of a fashionable furniture showroom, and again — she gasped — in Marge's gift shop, holding open an ornate photo album.

123

★ ★ ★

While Gracie checked from various seats in the choir loft, Pastor Paul experimented in positioning the beautiful stand. "Perfect," she said, at last. "No one will have to crane their neck to see Barb there."

"Or you," he said.

The search for Barb's elusive arrangement had taken a bit longer than anticipated, but when at length the faxing process was accomplished, Pastor Paul returned the original to Barb's crowded files, where it had turned out to be. Meanwhile Gracie went out to the kitchen.

Since she and Pastor Paul had conducted their treasure search, two items had appeared. Someone had propped a folded piece of lined paper against her handbag. Not another clue, she thought. Our swaps-thief is working overtime. But "Try this" was scrawled, rather than printed, with a nearly indecipherable recipe within.

"Hmmm." She scanned it quickly. She'd made bread of many varieties, but never with this particular combination of ingredients. "I'll do it," she promised aloud, "whoever you are."

The other addition should have been expected, after the lollipop appearance. A lovely, flared crystal vase held a spray of red carnations, interspersed with money plant — last year's crop, at least, since the stems held the opalescent "coins," rather than green leaves.

And there was a note. Opening it, Gracie read:

THE LOLLIPOPS YOU CONSPIRD
    TO KEEP.
(WHEN   YOU   CHEAT   THE
    CHILDREN, HOW CAN YOU
    SLEEP?)
NOW TAKE WARNING! LISTEN
    AND HEAR!
SHOULD THIS VASE ON THE
    ALTAR NOT APPEAR,
YOU WILL FEEL MY FURY, NEVER
    FEAR!

Gracie shuddered.

"Gracie?"

She turned, and Pastor Paul hurried to her. "What's wrong? You're white as — the money plant," he finished weakly. "Just while we were upstairs?"

"And a recipe for me."

"It . . . sounds like Pierre."

"Possibly. At least the recipe could be."

"Two of them? How do they do it, without us hearing anything?" He sank to a chair. "This is beginning to get to me!"

"I believe it's supposed to." She handed him the latest note.

He read it twice before giving it back. "None of the others have sounded threatening."

"More lighthearted," she agreed. "And even this . . ." Her voice faded off. "Sounds joking — do you think?"

"Can we take the chance?"

"And what chance are we taking if we —"

"Do what it says?"

"What can of worms might we be opening?"

For long moments, as they sat silent, Gracie turned the note over and over in her hands. At last, making even herself nervous, she put it in her purse.

"Won't the flowers be dead, anyway, by Sunday?"

She hadn't thought of that. "Not the money plant. The carnations will. Unless —" She examined the petals of one. "They're artificial," she said.

"No kidding!" He sighed. "So . . . ?"

"The note just says the vase. It doesn't mention the flowers."

"Gracie, what's going on in that devious mind of yours?"

"I'm not quite sure. But just putting the vase there — with something entirely different in it — would be meeting the criterion, sort of. The letter of the law, but not the spirit."

She wondered if Abe had a story to cover that!

"I'm whipped." Marge sank to a kitchen chair and eyed the goodies Gracie was packing in clear plastic containers to be frozen until Saturday morning. "Maybe they won't all fit . . . ?"

Gracie handed her a still-warm sticky bun. "*Hmmm*. Heaven!"

Gracie poured two cups of tea and settled across from Marge. The house was infinitely quiet. Lacey had gone home, Uncle Miltie was napping on the couch, and Gooseberry was off on some jaunt with the recovered Charlotte.

"Marge, you know that brass music stand —"

Marge straightened, sloshing tea. "I forgot to tell you! Remember the price tag I had on it?"

The figure was as much as Gracie had spent for her platform rocker.

"Would you believe that someone paid thirty dollars more than I was asking?"

"*More!*" Gracie was more convinced than ever that Uncle Miltie couldn't be involved.

George Morgan was anything but a spend-thrift. "Who?" she asked.

"Who what?" Marge mumbled around a gooey bite. "Gracie, you've outdone your-self!" She licked crumbs from her fingers.

"Who *bought* the music stand?"

"Haven't the faintest."

"You don't know who bought it?"

"Exactly." Marge propped her elbows on the table. "It was the strangest thing. I never saw him."

"You're certain it was a man?"

"Well, of course not — since I never saw the person."

"I don't understand."

Marge explained carefully, "I'd gone to the storeroom — you know, to start making room to unpack stuff."

Gracie nodded.

"And you know what it's like back there! Nothing ever where you expect it —"

"And that's when someone came and bought the music stand?"

"It must be. I'm certain it was there ear-lier. And I found the album closed and on the window seat. I'd never put it there!"

"But you saw no one."

"Nor heard anyone. Nor the door opening and closing, though I had thought there might have been a bit of a draft —"

"And when you came back from the store-room —" Gracie prompted.

"I found the money stacked neatly on the counter, and a printed note."

"All in capitals."

"Oh!" Marge pressed one set of fingertips to her lips. "You think —"

"Pastor Paul and I found your music stand when we were looking for an arrangement for Barb."

Marge shuddered delicately. "It's all a bit spooky, if you ask me. Things appearing and disappearing, strange notes, some person getting in and out and never being seen." She shrugged. "I . . . don't suppose you could spare another sticky bun . . . ?"

7

Wednesday mid-afternoon, Gracie thumped the sifter onto the counter. A small cloud of flour erupted, and Marge jumped back with a startled *"Wh—"*

"Sorry," Gracie said, "but I've had enough cooking for today. Have a cup of tea with me?"

"I thought you'd never ask!" Marge wiped her forehead with the hem of her apron, and Gracie didn't mention the interesting markings left across her makeup.

They nested on stools while the kettle ticked with heat.

Gracie plucked a brownie chip from the table. Marge asked, "How are we doing, Gracie?"

"Not bad, really. The chicken breasts and braised steaks are all in the freezer. And the breads and rolls. Tish and Tyne will help Friday with last-minute things. Barb, too, if she feels rested enough, though tonight's choir practice may do her in. Tomorrow I'll wash containers, check tablecloths and other supplies." Gracie needed to leave preparation of all of the salads for Friday afternoon or Saturday morning, to insure ultimate freshness. "How does the rest of the week look for you?"

"Tomorrow I need to be at the shop. All day. Since we're quitting early, I'll go for an hour or two yet this afternoon."

The kettle whistled, and Gracie hurried to lift it. The two friends sat at the table to enjoy a break, which ended all too soon.

"I've got to go," Marge said, rinsing her cup at the sink. "I'll see you at choir practice this evening."

"Before you go," Gracie said, not looking up, "you might want to check your makeup in the mirror." If Marge should meet anyone, even a meter reader, not looking her best, Gracie might well lose her best friend and neighbor to cardiac arrest.

I should be baking pies, Gracie told both herself and the Lord, as she slipped into her walking shoes. But I'm starting to feel as though I've been born and raised in this kitchen. *Lord, I've shorted my praise-walk every day this week so far . . . and while I guess my muscles can live with a little less exercise, I'm not sure my spirit can. There's something about our talks that brings things into focus, just as that dear child Lacey said. Lord, be with her and her grandmother —*

Her thought broke off as she remembered she had meant to stop by the newspaper office, to check something that had been nudging at the back of her mind. She knew she should be remembering something specific about Gillian Pomeroy. She could easily drop in there on her way.

It was a wonderful day for walking! Already, the temperature was cooling, and a soft breeze stirred grass, tree foliage and Gooseberry's elevated tail. It never failed to amaze Gracie how expressive that appendage was — how she could read her cat's mood or intentions by its posture, by its slightest flick, even.

Now, it seemed, he had sighted something of interest. That might mean anything from an unusual beetle to a cache of booty lost by bank robbers. Nothing would surprise Gracie where Gooseberry's finds were concerned.

"You're a fine cat!" She stooped closer to pet-level as he galloped toward her, a scrap of paper dangling from his mouth. She couldn't help but smile at his strange running gait — his legs seeming nearly elastic, his pads hitting with the softest of thumps. "Yes, Gooseberry," she crooned, smoothing his fur and receiving his purring acceptance. Charlotte gave Marge adulation; acceptance was as far as Gooseberry would go. But his acceptance was more than sufficient.

The paper fell from his mouth. Looking up at her, he touched it with a paw.

"If you say so, Gooseberry," she humored him. Then her eyes widened — not because what was obviously a short grocery list also held Gracie's own phone number, but because the list — shampoo, chocolates, tissues and apple juice — was printed in block characters identical to those on the ransom notes left at Eternal Hope Community Church!

"Gracie!" Rocky came to meet her, both hands extended to catch hers in his firm grip. "What a surprise! I thought you'd be up to your neck in meatloaf tettrazini, or pheasant fricassee, or some such delicacy!"

She made a wry face.

"You! Tired of cooking?" He laughed so heartily that his colleagues turned to look, then, smiling, went back to work. "I can understand, though," he said, taking her arm and leading her toward his office. "I love my job, but there are times when — if I had his portrait — I'd throw darts at Gutenberg himself." He waved her to a seat. "Now, what can I do for you?"

"I want to search . . . some files."

"The morgue," he translated.

She winced at the word.

"How far back?"

She sighed. "I guess I don't really know. There's a woman at Pleasant Haven whose condition doesn't seem right to me." She would have said more, been more specific, but she knew better than to voice unbacked suspicions in Rocky's presence. "Gillian Pomeroy. The name rings such a bell —"

He was leaning forward, elbows on his desk. "To me, too," he said. "Three years ago? Or maybe more. I took some photos. Some kind of rally, with a lot of posters jabbing the air, and shouts — and she . . . *she was the ringleader!* She was arrested, I believe! Come!" He was giant steps ahead of her, racing toward the room she still refused to call a morgue.

First he opened a huge file that moved easily on some kind of bearings, sagging only slightly at its full extension. His fingertips pranced over a few bulging manila envelopes, then selected one. "PROTEST MARCHES, etc." was block-printed with a wide black marker. Not nearly as neat as the ransom notes, she thought. If they found their thief, perhaps they could get him a job at the *Mason County Gazette* — keep him busy and out of mischief.

Making satisfied grunts, Rocky went to a long, scarred oak table and laid out the envelope's contents. "She's here!" he said. "Not just once. Here . . . and here . . . and here —"

"Rocky," came over the loudspeaker, "the commissioner's on line one."

He sighed. "What's new?" he muttered, then said, "I'm sorry, Gracie. I'll be back as soon as I can. In the meantime —" He gestured to the daunting mass of newspaper clippings.

Gracie settled into a straight-backed chair and told herself she wasn't going to get caught up in any of this. All she needed was a bit of background, in order to understand a little better where Lacey's grandmother had come from. Not geographically, of course. She knew that was Mason City. But rather, ideologically. Philosophically.

Despite her intentions, she found herself intrigued.

During a march with Mothers Against Drunk Driving, the camera had caught Gillian Pomeroy dressed as Carrie Nation, carrying a hatchet, at tomahawk stance.

Isn't that a bit of overkill, Lord? she asked.

135

Still, she had to smile. The woman made her point.

Suddenly, a memory recurred with perfect clarity — she and Elmo at Abe's deli, a newspaper spread between them. Could it have been this very one? She was almost certain — yes! totally certain — that it had involved Gillian Pomeroy. . . .

"The woman annoys me," El had said. "Anyone who goes overboard does. But — sorry, dear — I think it wears worse on a woman." His hand covered hers, and she didn't pull away, even though such a remark was uncharacteristic.

" 'The hand that rocks the cradle,' " Abe quoted. "The nurturer, rather than one who accomplishes?"

El shifted. "Women . . . do both. Nurture and accomplish." He added. "At least women like Gracie do."

"And what should we do with this Pomeroy woman — who annoys my friend Elmo Parks? And, apparently, many others, since she was hauled off to jail for it."

"*We* don't do anything. But her husband should chain her to the kitchen stove."

It was then that Gracie withdrew her hand.

"Tell me, my friend," Abe continued thoughtfully, "in our small area of Indiana

— how many were killed by drunk drivers this past year?"

El hesitated. "Four, maybe."

"And the year before that?"

"About the same. And the year before that, too," he added hurriedly, as though to forestall a third asking of the question. "What's the point?"

"Be patient, my friend. We are only halfway there. Now. How often has this particular group marched? These mothers troubled by drunk driving?"

El frowned. "I guess I never noticed before."

"But you notice now?"

Grudgingly, El said, "I guess everyone notices now."

"Exactly. When we want to make a dent in heads and hearts of stone, we seldom use a feather-duster. We choose instead a chisel and mallet."

"Or a hatchet." Elmo tapped the newspaper. "I get your point, Abe. And I think I'm beginning to get hers."

At that, Gracie placed her hand over El's. . . .

Looking at the clipping, reliving the scene, she could almost sense the warmth of the moment.

"Are you finding what you need?"

Gracie started.

"I frightened you."

"No. I was a million miles away."

"The morgue does that to me, too." He sank into the chair opposite her. The overhead lights, she noticed, glinted in his silvering hair. "It's living history. How far have you gotten into your research?"

She laughed. "Only this one story."

"The tip of the iceberg, it seems." He extracted a clipping with the headline, "Who Wears the Fur Here, Anyway?" A four-column-wide photo showed a woman in a cartoon-like fox costume holding off her pursuers with a toy bazooka. The caption identified the "fox" as Gillian Pomeroy.

Gracie found three additional stories in which Lacey's grandmother figured prominently. In each case, news photos showed her dressed dramatically in some way that guaranteed her message would be noted.

"It's all coming back," Rocky said. "She's a newsman's dream — or nightmare, depending. And you say she's — ill?"

"There was an accident. A fall. Now she requires constant care."

"Sad. You're sure it was an accident?"

"Her daughter and son-in-law are, yes." She knew that this was the point where she must be on guard — that point where friendship took a back seat to a cautious awareness of the reporter's nose.

He leaned forward. "But . . . *you're* not certain?"

"Rocky, be reasonable! I don't know enough about the woman to make any judgment!"

"Because," he said, watching her closely, "there's a more recent piece of news I didn't remember until I was talking with the commissioner just now."

He waited.

She braced.

"A couple of months ago," he said slowly, "Pomeroy headed a march against a chemical company that wanted to displace a historic cemetery — move it grave by grave a mile or so."

Gracie shuddered.

"Just this past week, the plans were set in motion again. It just occurred to me — maybe the main adversary was conveniently removed."

The Eternal Hope choir, including guest singer Eudora McAdoo, was abuzz with conjecture about the sudden appearance of the spectacular brass music stand. And Gracie could scarcely blame them. The overhead lights sparked blinding flares in the curved tubular base and glanced across the carved upper section where Barb had already placed music.

"It's beautiful!" Lacey had accepted Gracie's and Uncle Miltie's invitations to join them at practice. "Is it real gold?"

"We should use it every single Sunday!" Tyne declared.

"Yes," echoed Tish. "It would be selfish not to share it!"

"It's certainly a thousand percent more endurable than that other monstrosity!"

"I beg your pardon, Estelle!" Lester Twomley elevated his chin, and of course the rest of his face went along. "That music stand is a family heirloom."

"About as venerable as my grandfather's old stuffed possum! Mercy, Les! Why not bring in a box of rubbed-out school chalk erasers?"

"Please." Barb tried again, but not as though she entertained any real hope of attention.

"Poor little fingers calloused, tiny lips bleeding —" Estelle continued.

Lester looked stony.

Lacey's eyes were wide and wounded. "Are they always this mean?" she whispered close to Gracie's ear, "in a church?"

Unable to think of a reasonable response, Gracie just gave the child a quick hug. No one was retreating, it seemed, and Gracie was about to intervene when Amy Cantrell said gently, "Well, I always enjoyed Mr. Twomley's story myself!" Then several of the others echoed her sentiments — out of affection for Lester if not out of any respect for the historical or sentimental value of his boyhood memento.

Please, Lord, she prayed as the hubbub continued on all sides, *keep this sweet child from seeing us at our very worst. In this choir family, help us all to remember that we're not here to be first, or loudest, or best — and certainly we're not here to show cleverness or hurtfulness, but rather love. Love for You, Lord. And how can we possibly reflect and return Your love if we don't love one another?*

The controversy continued, though on a milder, more impersonal note.

"Who would give us such a lovely, lovely thing? Who could *afford* to?"

Don Delano asked, "Was it all that expensive, Marge?"

"Expensive enough."

"And you never saw who bought it? Not even a glimpse?" Estelle raised an eyebrow. "I do find that hard to believe!"

"Well, it's true!" Marge insisted.

141

"Oh, I didn't mean —"

"Yes you did, Estelle."

"People, please!" Barb's baton thunked on the brass stand.

"Don't bang it, Barb! You'll ding it!"

"That's one thing about that one of mine," Les said. "You could use it without being afraid of damage."

"How would it show? It was so battered already!"

Barb slumped to the front pew, her head in her hands.

"Excuse me," Gracie said, and left the loft to sit at Barb's side. "Would you mind if I directed, Barb, while you played? Since you're so tired. . . ." She lowered her voice. "And since the natives seem restless tonight."

"It's the full moon," Barb said. "It must be!"

More likely, Gracie thought, it was all the suspense surrounding the brass stand, and the other unexplained events. She tugged on Barb's arm, and before long pages were rustling, throats clearing and the choir ready for serious business. *Finally!*

By the time they had run through Sunday's anthem — an easy arrangement of "The Old Rugged Cross" — and practiced a few staples from their repertoire for those who could participate in Pleasant Haven's Family Day, good humor seemed restored.

Gracie felt Barb showed great wisdom — or a strong sense of self-preservation — by saying that they'd save for some future evening the difficult anthem that had excited such furor at the previous practice.

Lacey seemed to have aroused Estelle's "mother hen" instinct, for she had taken the child under her wing, declaring her own "considerable experience with professional instruction." Rather than feeling annoyance, Gracie breathed a sigh of relief. In the presence of such talent — especially in the high soprano range — Estelle tended to be territorial. So it came as a surprise to everyone, it seemed, when Estelle insisted that Lacey be given a solo, especially since her grandmother would be in the Saturday audience. Lacey stuttered a protest, but her face glowed as those who stood near resoundingly seconded the motion.

"How do you feel about that, dear?" Barb asked.

"If you included a few other solos," Estelle suggested silkily, "Lacey might feel less alone."

At once Barb said, "What a fine idea! Rick, you could do that wonderful 'Ten Thousand Angels.' And Amy — that solo you did a few weeks back?" She turned to Lacey. "Have you ever done a solo, dear?"

"Singing to Gram, but not to real people." She flushed. "I mean, Gram is real, but —"

"But you mean real people who are also strangers. Why don't you try us?" Barb suggested with a smile. "We're real people."

Amy suggested shyly, "Could Lacey do 'He's Got the Whole World in His Hands'? I just loved that song when I was young!"

There were ripples of fond laughter. Compared to most of them, Amy was *still* extremely young!

"I know that one!" Lacey said. "Gram taught me."

"Then we have it!" Barb said decisively. "And we'll all sing it with you, first time through. Later, then, everyone else will sit in the front pew, so Lacey gets the feeling of an audience."

Amy found copies, and Gracie — one hand on Lacey's arm for support — felt the child's body trembling. She could sympathize — but then so could most of the remainder of humanity. Unexpectedly, she remembered Arlen, the first time he was to recite a Bible verse in the Vacation Bible School program. She'd wondered then, as now, *Is it fair, Lord, to afflict them with these expectations?* But the answer had come — either His or hers, she couldn't be certain — that if children didn't learn to cope with stage fright at an early age, instead of defeating it they would learn to avoid circumstances where they might share talents — and faith — and so lose much of the richness life offers.

Lacey leaned into Gracie's touch, and the trembling continued, shaking her voice for the first few phrases. But then the child straightened, even moved forward a step, and her glorious voice rang confidently, unfalteringly, the others undergirding and surrounding it.

Gracie sang softly.

So did everyone else.

Lacey clutched her book, not looking up as the door at the rear of the sanctuary burst open and her aunt — disheveled and agitated — stumbled down the center aisle.

All other voices stopped — Estelle's in mid-screech — and Lacey's faltered. Then, buoyed by Barb's encouraging "Keep going, dear," and Gracie's hand on her shoulder, she sang on — apparently oblivious of everyone, mildly embarrassed, but with such an angelic quality that all the choir members — like one multi-headed body — lost interest in the interruption and turned to listen raptly.

It was only as the song ended that applause erupted and Lacey looked up. *"Aunt Kelly!"* she thrust her small hand into Gracie's.

"Lace," the woman said, her voice harsh. "You've got to come. She's *worse*. She's at the hospital, in intensive care."

8

Gracie slowed her steps to accommodate Uncle Miltie's pace on the highly waxed tile floor of the hospital corridor. The walker might not slip, but she could see his tension nonetheless. "What's wrong with carpet?" he grumbled. "The outdoor kind — *anything* that doesn't act like an Olympic skating rink." He was in one of those periods when his osteoarthritis slowed him down more than he had the patience for.

Lacey, huddled dispiritedly on a coral-colored molded chair, jumped up and ran to greet them. "They won't let me see her! They call it 'I-see-you' — but they don't mean it."

Gracie hunkered down to accept her tearful hug. "ICU means Intensive Care Unit, honey. Is your aunt with her now? I think they limit visitors to one at a time."

Lacey shrugged. "The one nice nurse said maybe later. Just for a minute." She clung desperately as they walked together to the cluster of chairs.

"Did they say what had happened? Another fall?"

"Just medicine, I think. Too much or too little —" She shrugged. "What difference does it make? Either way, God's not keeping His promise. I could've done better with . . . *the Tooth Fairy!*" Her voice caught on a sob. "And I haven't believed in *her* for years and years!"

Gracie caught her close. "Don't give up on God, dear. Not ever."

"But things get worse and worse! If I keep depending on Him — Gram might die!"

Oh, dear Lord, how do I tell her that Gram might die in any event? That You don't promise us immortality on Earth, only the strength to keep us sturdy so that we spend Eternity with You — and offer us all those wonderful, wonderful blessings in the meantime? Once again, she felt a nudging — a feeling stronger than suspicion, yet not quite as firm as certainty — that she was on the verge of discovering something for herself, and for Lacey. That God was depending on her to use the gifts of perception He had given her —

"Now, dear," a nurse was saying. "Just for a few minutes." To Gracie and Uncle Miltie, she said, "Would you like to watch through the window?"

Uncle Miltie tried to get up but his shoes slipped, and when Gracie offered a hand, he waved her on.

Through the large plate-glass window, she saw Lacey leaning toward Gillian Pomeroy. She held her grandmother's limp hand in her own. Although Lacey's lips moved, no sound penetrated the glass.

The nurse said softly, "She's singing."

Gracie blinked tears. Would it be "A Dream Is a Wish Your Heart Makes" or —

" 'He's Got the Whole World in His Hands'," the nurse said. "We tend to forget that here."

"We tend to forget that — everywhere," Gracie amended, then asked, "Are you allowed to tell me — what happened?"

The nurse's lips firmed. "Somebody," she said tightly, "messed up on her medication. It's just lucky we reached her when we did." She sighed. "Or . . . maybe it wasn't luck. Maybe it was *Him*."

Blinking back tears, Gracie turned to see Uncle Miltie and Lacey's Aunt Kelly perched on opposing chairs, but as solitary as though neither was aware of the other. Uncle Miltie glared the length of the corridor, so polished that reflections of the overhead lights blazed a path. Kelly stared into space, the lines of her face drawn far beyond her years. *How old was she?* Gracie wondered. There was a vulnerability that spoke of the late twenties, when she was relaxed — yet a world-weariness that made her seem older than Uncle Miltie.

The young woman jerked around, suddenly focused, rigid, hands tightening convulsively on her purse. At first Gracie felt guilt for having studied her so closely. But Kelly's gaze swept beyond and behind Gracie, far down the corridor, where a tall, dark figure approached with long strides. As he drew closer, his features revealed themselves, and Kelly stood, woodenly, and held her hands before her. Not to receive an embrace, Gracie felt, but more as one would ward off a blow.

Grif Ransen flicked a glance toward Gracie, then turned his hard eyes on Kelly. "Not even a note to tell me where to find my supper?"

"I'm sorry, Grif, honey."

"You just leave that old bat to tell me — when you know she can't tell straight up unless it has to do with that monstrosity she owns?"

"Mrs. Fountain did tell you, though — she must have, since you're here."

"Here and starved."

"Grif, honey, there was no time —" She

shrank back, lifting her arms as though to shield her face.

But Grif would not strike her, Gracie knew. Not here. Not with witnesses.

Dear Lord, she prayed silently, *I can't even imagine what it would be like to fear a husband. Elmo was such a dear, loving man — difficult, at times, but aren't we all? And his love was strong and sweet and encompassing, always a protector, never a threat.*

And I still miss him, she thought. And she always would. But the poet who'd written " 'Tis better to have loved and lost . . ." knew what he was talking about. *Lord, You know I cherished every moment with El — and don't begrudge his being with You now — but I truly do miss that man!*

"They called from the hospital," Kelly whispered intensely. "I only had time to tell Miss Cordelia where I'd be . . . and pick up Lacey —"

"You had time to chitchat with the old bat — *and* time to pick up your sister's brat — but no time to set out some sandwiches —"

"Grif, honey . . . she's my *mother!*" Her voice had become a wail. "And they said she might d-d-d—"

"The word is 'die,' " he finished coldly, avoiding her pleading hands. "And it's what we've wanted, isn't it?"

Stumbling backward, Kelly gasped, fist to her mouth.

Gracie longed to take her in her arms, but something restrained her. Perhaps it was the knowledge that it would only make things worse — if not now, later. In any event, the nurse appeared, leading Lacey by the hand, and indicated that Kelly could see her mother again.

Kelly turned, but Grif caught her arm and said roughly, "She's got to go home now!" He jerked his head toward Lacey.

Lacey set her face in stubborn lines, then looked at her aunt, sighed, and gave Gracie a good-bye squeeze. Gracie yearned to ask if the child could stay overnight with her and Uncle Miltie — but again, something held her back. Perhaps, with the child nearby, Grif wouldn't feel free to abuse his wife physically, as — even then — he battered her with his expression and his biting words.

Lord, Gracie confided as she and Gooseberry took Thursday morning's praise-walk at an accelerated pace, *I really don't have time for feeling at loose ends. What's wrong with me? If I'm going to feel frazzled, it had better be between the oven and the sink.*

Gooseberry tangled himself around her

ankles — she supposed with the aim of slowing her down.

She obliged, pausing to sit on a bit of stone wall abutting a bridge.

Her feline companion informed her that hadn't been his intention. Taking the hint, she rubbed him between the ears, and his head pressed hard into her palm. Dear Gooseberry, purring his contentment. Did he have any idea the peace he brought to her? *Lord, I praise You for the companionship of pets. We learn so much from their devotion.*

"Hello, again!" A car pulled beside her, its engine idling.

Gracie saw first the tangerine hair — perfectly matched to the pattern of silkscreened poppies rambling over a cream-colored jacket.

Eudora McAdoo's smile spread the same orange tone nearly the width of her face. "I hoped I'd find you walking again."

Disengaging Gooseberry from her ankles, Gracie stood. "And I should be about it."

"So much yet to do, I suppose, preparing for Saturday. Wait! I'll park the car and walk with you. The bathroom scales whimpered this morning."

Gracie set a good pace, and this time Eudora lagged only slightly behind. "And how is dear Milton this morning?" she asked, scarcely puffing.

"Actually, his name's George. Miltie's just a nickname. He was resting when Gooseberry and I left."

Gracie pumped her arms. A breeze picked up, carrying seductive scents of warming earth and fresh-cut grass.

"I'd be happy to help," Eudora ventured — in a tone Gracie knew was meant to appear casual — "with whatever it is you have to do today. For Saturday."

Just what I need, Gracie thought — but she didn't say it to God, Who would almost certainly find it unkind — *Eudora flirting underfoot.* She didn't have time to serve either as chaperone or as Uncle Miltie's buffer. "How kind of you to offer," she said, "but everything's covered."

Eudora sighed. "Just remember, then, any time you need me. . . ."

Eudora's enthusiasm for walking ended after less than a mile, once she had exhausted her questions and comments about "dear, funny Milton — er, George" and had taken Gracie on a verbal tour of the shops in Greece. Gooseberry, bored, defected at the first mention of terra cotta fragments turned into jewelry, though he stayed within hearing distance. While Gracie couldn't see him, she could see evidence of his passing in the rippling of taller grasses — which, Eudora said, shivering, took her back to that terrifying moment on her most recent safari when unseen lions had stalked the party. And this was the woman who yearned to visit Cleveland!

Lord, Gracie thought with an element of desperation, *I should be enthralled! Chances are, I'll never go on a safari, and I should store up every detail for Uncle Miltie for some rainy day when he's in a* National Geographic *mood. And Marge would be delighted hearing about that jewelry — I wonder if Eudora ever happened to jot down the name of a Greek distributor from whom she could order direct. But, Lord, I have* so *much to think about, so much to do. . . .*

". . . turn back," Eudora was saying — but not in a hurt way, as though she'd perceived Gracie's wandering attention. "Since you can't use me today, I'll take the car for a wash, and maybe get my nails done. Perhaps even eat out. Where would you suggest?"

"Abe Wasserman's deli," Gracie said without hesitation, and gave directions. "And if you have time . . . my friend Marge Lawrence, who runs a gift shop, would love to hear what you were just telling me —

about the crafts and jewelry you found in Greece."

"Oh? Delightful! Now do remember me to your adorable uncle!" With a jaunty wave, she was on her way.

Gracie breathed an inward sigh of relief, and — within minutes — Gooseberry marched ahead of her, tail once again proudly aloft.

"I can't possibly settle down," Gracie told Gooseberry, "until I stop by Cordelia Fountain's and see if she knows anything more about Lacey and her grandmother." And, she couldn't help admitting to herself, she was concerned as well about Kelly. "But not Grif," she said firmly. "Even God must find it hard to love him."

How can You, Lord? Perhaps You find his sins just a few shades blacker than those the remainder of us are guilty of. But what makes a person so heartless? And selfish, too. Yes, I know, we're all self-centered, and I guess You might even say that what I feel toward that young man reveals my own heartlessness. Forgive me, Lord, for being judgmental. Please cover Lacey and her grandmother with Your protective love — and Kelly, as well. She surely needs it, married to that man —

And she *was* being judgmental again. To

keep herself from thinking, she turned on her cassette player and sang along with some favorite gospel hymns. Before she knew it, she was within view of Fountain's Tourist Home — a truly lovely, stately old home, green-shuttered, its white wood siding gleaming in sunlight where not shaded by trees older than any citizen in Willow Bend.

Cordelia was on her knees beside one of the flower beds, weeding among the begonias. She pushed the brim of a floppy straw hat back from her eyes. Fingerstreaks of dirt proved that it had been bothering her for some time.

"Cordelia," Gracie greeted, while Gooseberry found a toad to harrass. "You look like a picture from a fashion book of long ago."

Well, not quite, Gracie amended in her thoughts. The ribbon-tied straw hat fit, but the T-shirt with Van Gogh scenes front and back didn't quite make it, nor did the frayed baggy denims, white socks and old tennis shoes.

Cordelia settled back, giving the hat brim one last vicious tug. "I try to keep up appearances, when I'm expecting new people — but I kept tripping over my long skirt, and I thought — closer to the time they arrive, I could skitter back into the house and change into something more in keeping with the period."

"You're expecting someone special?" Gracie sat on the tire swing, and pushed gently back and forth.

"All of my guests are special, Gracie, you know that. Except —" she glanced toward the second story, and primped her lips shut. "The child's delightful, she truly is, but her aunt is an enigma, if you ask me, and that man —"

"Grif?"

"What kind of name is Grif, I ask you! If I'd seen him first, I can assure you, I'd have found some reason to refuse them. Say the place is haunted, or something. You know, of course, about the tunnel used as part of the Underground Railroad?"

"That is so exciting!" Gracie said. "I never tire of hearing of it! But I wondered —"

Cordelia attacked another weed. "He — the uncle — looks as though he'd run if he thought there were ghosts! Those big, pushy ones are always just cowards at heart. It was a sad day when he got a full-time job here — right in Willow Bend."

"Oh?"

"At Pleasant Haven, hadn't you heard? He's in grounds maintenance or something,

I guess. But if he doesn't do any more there than he does around here —"

Gracie waited, to see if the sentence would continue. When it didn't, she asked, "Have you heard anything further about the mother?"

Cordelia pushed to her feet. Her knees were wet and muddy, but Gracie still wished she could find time this weekend to do some of her own gardening. Who could resist the feel of wet earth, and the smell of growing things? Not she. She loved muddy knees.

"She nearly died," Cordelia confided. "I felt so sorry for the child. It's such a responsibility, being an innkeeper, wanting to keep your distance — give clients their privacy — and yet just aching to hug some of them. Of course, I'd happily put poison in the breakfast eggs of a few others."

Gracie felt certain she knew who the current nominee for a toxic breakfast would be.

"Well, this morning, the hospital called again, and then the woman and child were off again. They were looking more chipper by a sight than yesterday. Not wanting to pry, I didn't ask, but the child ran over and asked if she could please take a geranium from the window box for her grandmother, that she was sure she'd be well enough today to enjoy it. So of course, I said she could, as long as it was a little one — and from the back where it wouldn't show."

The interview with Cordelia having done little to settle her nerves, Gracie decided to stop in briefly at Abe's deli for a cup of hot lemon tea. If she happened to run into Eudora there, she'd fake amnesia — or maybe madness, like David in that one Bible scene.

Come to think of it, madness might not be such a stretch, if things kept on going as they were.

Eudora wasn't there, but Amy was working, and Gracie already felt better. Amy didn't seem her usual sunny self, though, and the reason soon became apparent. "I don't understand her!" she said. "She can be so sweet — like she was with Lacey — and a minute later she gets really nasty!"

Estelle Livett, of course.

Amy knelt on the chair opposite Gracie and leaned across the table. "Do you suppose she's one of those people with multiple personalities?" Without waiting for an answer, she plopped into the chair and confided, "I talked to Mr. Wasserman about it —"

"About what, sweet Amy?" Abe joined them, setting down his mug of congealing coffee even as he settled into a chair. "About what did we speak? Estelle?"

Amy nodded.

"And I offered my pearls of wisdom, as ever — but they seem not to have sufficed. Why is that?"

Amy folded and refolded a napkin. "I know that you're right, and that we should, like you said, 'judge our neighbor with justice.' "

"Leviticus," Abe said, smiling toward Gracie. "We share that, you and I."

"And that other thing you quoted —"

"From the Talmud." He nodded. "We do not share that, at least not directly."

"Tell Gracie what it says?"

" 'Judge the whole of a person favorably.' It means simply that we must not isolate a few moments from time and base our assessment on that only. The total person must be considered, good as well as bad, the totality of his or her life, the broad spectrum of moods and relationships and causative features. Since my own judgment is fallible — and the Talmud does not, I think, say this — I tend to weigh quite heavily on the good, even to the point of injustice on that side of the balance."

"Judge as you would be judged," Gracie contributed.

"Exactly!" He threw back his head and laughed. "When the time of my judgment comes, I would appreciate having my overwhelming weaknesses shrunken, and those few strengths I possess magnified!"

Amy reached out to touch his hand. "That's not true! You're one of the best people I know! Isn't he, Gracie?"

"He's one of the best I know, without doubt," Gracie agreed.

"And if this should someday be true," he said quietly, reaching for each of their hands and joining all at the center of the table, "is it not because I am wise enough to choose good people as my friends?"

Their hands remained clasped for a time, then he released them and pushed away from the table. "But now — time for work! Sweet Amy, bring my friend here whatever she desires — even to the half of my kingdom!"

Hot tea, of whatever flavor, possessed great curative powers, and so Gracie decided to make one more stop before returning home.

Gooseberry had long since gone his own way, so she had no one to report to or ask for permission except herself. Briskly, she walked the short distance to Marge's gift shop.

Marge had set a small display on the sidewalk in front of the store, and Gracie paused for a moment, enjoying its color and movement. A rack of filmy scarves and shawls from India moved entrancingly with the slightest breeze. Their rainbow tones formed constantly changing patterns. Gracie watched as a child about two or three years of age ran over and immersed herself among the filmy fabrics, while her mother, panic-stricken, rushed to draw her back.

From the doorway, Marge said, "Don't worry about her. I feel the same way about soft fabrics. In fact, I remember as a child crawling into my mother's closet and stroking my face with the skirts of her dresses."

The woman smiled. "You're unusually understanding." And to her child, she said, "At least, honey, give me your ice cream cone."

It was too late, of course. Chocolate smeared a caftan swirled with colors of the sea.

"Oh, dear." The mother reached for her purse. "How much is it?" There was something about the way she clutched the purse to her that translated the lines of worry in her face.

Marge said, "I wouldn't think of it! It's

not really your color. And whenever I put temptation on the sidewalk, I expect the occasional accident." She pulled the stained article from the display. "See? It scarcely shows. I'm certain I can get it out."

"Can you?" Gracie asked, once the woman had expressed gratitude a dozen different ways and hauled her child away.

Marge grinned. "With a scissors." She shrugged. "I was looking for a reason to take it myself. Now I have it." As they entered the cool dimness of the store, she added, "Guess who came by today."

"Eudora McAdoo?"

Marge threw her a startled look, then shrugged. "She said you'd suggested it. And thanks! She bought two scented candles, a scarf and some costume jewelry. Too bad I don't sell hair color to match!"

Tablecloths, napkins, tableware, styrofoam cups and serving plates and bowls — all were packed. Uncle Miltie had scouted the flower beds to see what might be at peak readiness Saturday morning for cutting and arranging in milkglass vases — or, if Gracie preferred, he said, some of the pottery pieces she'd bought from local crafters. "Maybe it would bring them some business. Some of those Pleasant Haven dwellers use fifties to light their candles. They might be tempted to spend it, instead."

When she looked askance, he said, "So I exaggerate. Glads — as many as you want. The Peace and Lincoln roses look just about right — and there are some of those big white hosta blooms, if you want them."

"And Queen Anne's lace," she added. Despite his disdain, she'd insisted that several clumps near the rose garden be left unmown. Since they also benefited from the plant food she gave the flowers, they were tall and abundantly flowered, some blooms a full five inches in diameter.

"If you want weeds," he sniffed.

"God created weeds, too."

"He also created mosquitos and Japanese beetles — though I don't notice you inviting *them* in the house."

It was one of the few areas of disagreement between them. It amazed her that someone so perceptive and sensitive could fail to see the intricate beauty of roadside "weeds" like blue chicory, milkweed, Queen Anne's lace (she refused to call it wild carrot!) and even dandelions.

"First thing Saturday, I'll take care of the centerpieces — if you want me to."

She gave him a quick hug. "You're a sweetheart."

"Who says?" he grumped.

She nearly replied, "Eudora McAdoo, for one," but she didn't want him to go into cardiac arrest.

He punched her arm lightly. "You're pretty nice yourself, for a niece. What are you up to this afternoon?"

"I think I'll try a new recipe," she said. "Multigrain bread."

He grunted. "Something disgustingly good for me, I suppose."

"Or surprisingly good-tasting! I got it from a chef . . . I think."

He raised a quizzical eyebrow. "You *think* he's a chef, or —"

"I mean I think I know where it came from. It was left at the church. Anonymously."

He shook his head. "If you ask me, there's a lot of strange goings-on at that church. Should change its name from Eternal Hope to Infernal Interlopers — with such peculiar comings and goings." He headed off — his walker stomping before him — and arranged himself for a nap on the couch.

Assembling honey, oil, three kinds of flour, oatmeal, oat bran, almonds, wheat berries, sesame and sunflower seeds, raisins, dried cranberries and endless other possible ingredients, Gracie soon lost herself in her work. *This is when I come alive, Lord,* she confided — not that He didn't know that better than she ever could. She broke the packets of dry yeast into warm water. *This is when I feel a closeness to Your people all down through the centuries — for if ever anything binds us together, it's bread.*

She could close her eyes and imagine biblical women gathering grapes and spreading them on nets to dry in the sun — raisins to be eaten with their bread, hot from the stone oven. And what about the Indian and Mexican mothers and wives painstakingly grinding corn, stone against hollowed-out stone, while flies buzzed and lizards slithered, and the merciless Southwestern sun beat down, heating their surroundings to shimmering mirages? Or the New England pioneers, knuckles reddened and itchy from cold, shoes and knitted hose and homespun hems wet through as they scooped vibrant cranberries from the surface of autumn-cold bogs?

And we go to a store, Lord, and grumble if we have to wait a day for something to come in on the grocery truck.

She put the dough hook on her mixer, and was just reaching for the plug when the door vibrated with a firm knock.

Not Lacey, she knew — or Amy Cantrell

— or Marge. The first two knocked like butterflies beating their wings, and Marge — when she bothered to knock at all — tapped like an undernourished woodpecker.

Wiping her floury hands on her apron, she was on her way to answer when the door burst open and Pierre accosted her, hands on his hips. "You must grind your own flour!" he accused. "*Always,* grain must be hand-ground. Look at this . . . this abomination!" He thumped on the bags of whole wheat and cracked wheat flours until tan clouds rose. "And you're using a mixer? A *mixer!* For my special *pain complet?* Even an idiot knows that the fingertips must stroke the ingredients, blending them sensitively. There must be that — that — that marriage of fingertip and dough —"

Holding his head in his hands, he plunked himself onto a stool and regarded her with stormy eyes. "Had I known you were an infidel —"

"What's going on?" Uncle Miltie demanded with as much authority as he could summon when not fully awake. His eyes squinted, he hadn't put on his glasses and his scant hair stood in wild gray wisps.

"And you are?" Pierre demanded haughtily.

"He lives here," Gracie said, struggling

168

between temper and laughter. She simply must restore some element of decorum to her kitchen. "George Morgan, this is —"

"I *know* who this is!" Uncle Miltie thumped his walker on kitchen tile. "He's the ex-chef who thinks he can come into our home and insult my niece!"

"Sir, you should instruct your niece in the way a proper cook approaches her tasks. You should train her to respect the gifts of nature — and use them only in their purest forms. Only see here —" He nudged the bottle of oil. "Is this olive oil, pressed by Italian craftsmen from olives still warm from the grove? *No!* Not even olive oil brutalized by machinery! Vegetable oil! *Pure* vegetable oil, its label announces pretentiously! Pure *nonsense!* You have created anarchy, Madame! Surely — *surely,* I noted on the recipe —" He snatched the card and studied his scrawlings. Laying it down more gently, he said, "Nonetheless, you should have surmised — nay, you should have known with infallible certitude —"

Gooseberry chose that moment to peer from the living-room doorway.

"And a cat!" Pierre sneered. "In a kitchen!"

"Not in," Uncle Miltie huffed. "And not just an ordinary cat! Gooseberry — Goose-

169

berry —" he sputtered, then finished definitely, "This cat has credentials every bit as good as yours — and his manners are a darned sight better!"

"Mmmm." Pierre's attention seemed to have wandered — not far, just to a small bowl heaped with blond brownies. "May I?" he asked.

"Of course." Thinking that perhaps he'd forgotten his crusade against technology, Gracie started the mixer on low.

"Have one." Pierre extended the bowl to Uncle Miltie, who had mellowed to the point of sitting down.

"Don't mind if I do."

They chewed silently for at least five seconds.

"Wonderful as always, Gracie," Uncle Miltie said — as always.

Pierre exploded from his seat, his stool falling backward, striking the doorframe and missing Gooseberry only because the feline instinct for self-preservation was so perfected. *"Formidable,* my dear Madame!" he declared, swooping upon her and bestowing on her floury knuckles a kiss. "I *must* have the recipe!"

9

Pierre spread butter on a thick slab of the still-warm multigrain bread, took one bite, closed his eyes and murmured in ecstasy. "I *must* have the recipe —" he broke off. "But I guess I already do!"

Even Uncle Miltie joined in the laughter. Over the afternoon, working together, the three of them had developed a real camaraderie. Soon after his arrival, Gracie had convinced Pierre that he should call Pleasant Haven to reassure them of his safety. She then took the phone and firmly promised that after dinner Uncle Miltie and she would return him. "I wonder, though," she asked, "if he'd like, could we borrow him and his culinary skills again tomorrow?"

Pierre, listening in, clasped his hands and gave a childlike squeal. "Yes, yes, *yes!*" he whispered, bouncing a little on the balls of his feet.

Gracie turned with a smile. "They said it was fine."

"Probably be happy to be rid of him," Uncle Miltie had said, semi-grumpily.

"No doubt," Pierre agreed.

They worked together, making cranberry-apple-nut and lemon-poppyseed mini-muffins while the dough for crescent rolls advanced through its various stages. When Gracie suggested a break, Pierre helped Uncle Miltie clear just enough table space for three mugs.

"I'm a firm believer," Gracie said, only half in jest, "in the premise that if world leaders sat down with steaming mugs of tea, all bloodshed would cease."

And even though Uncle Miltie snorted fondly and Pierre raised a caustic eyebrow in a purely French manner, unquestionably *something* was working its magic in her kitchen. The wonderful baking scents issuing from the oven couldn't hurt, either.

"It occurs," Pierre said later — their friendship cemented and the rolls nearly too hot still to taste — "that perhaps flour already ground is permissible — but only when time is short."

"Of course," Gracie murmured.

"And your — machine." This admission seemed to come with great difficulty. "The . . . bread hook . . ."

"Of course we did the later kneading by hand," she pointed out.

His suffering seemed to ease.

"As my granddaddy used to say," Uncle Miltie contributed comfortably, "there's more than one way to skin a cat —" He broke off suddenly, as though just realizing what he'd said, and reached to stroke Gooseberry, now permitted in the kitchen since all baking for the day was ended.

"No offense," Uncle Miltie added, and Gooseberry seemed to take none.

For long moments they sat relaxed, content without conversation.

Although, Gracie directed her thoughts toward the Lord, *I do need to thank You for the way You worked things out here today. And for tomorrow, too. I'll admit, I was feeling a bit frantic — wondering what I'd do if Marge was unable to help, at least. I do that so often, don't I — talk a good faith, and then fuss as though I didn't have any at all. Pierre is such a sweet man — and genuinely talented. Could it be that if he helps here occasionally, he won't feel the need to keep running away? Whatever You have in mind, Lord, I know it will be fun to be a part of.*

And about Lacey and her family. You know best there, too — just as You always do. Help me to remember that and rest in Your wise and wonderful care. Amen.

While they still sat in companionable silence, Gooseberry meandered to the door, meowing a greeting.

"It smells absolutely *enticing* in here!" Marge called, letting herself in and Gooseberry out, then tapping on the door.

Pierre observed mildly, "Zeez Americans have — so you say — such strange customs. In Paree, we knock *before* entrance!"

Marge gasped. "I had no idea you had a guest —"

Pierre shrugged expressively. "A guest? I think not!"

Marge sidled closer to Gracie. "Isn't that —"

Gracie tugged her friend to a stool, in front of a section of table cluttered with ingredients. "Pierre has been teaching us secrets he learned apprenticing under master chefs." She stressed the final words with pats to Marge's arm.

"Ah."

"Experience is everything, and one never stops learning," Uncle Miltie informed her grandly.

"Let's hear it for the culinary arts!" Marge agreed.

Gracie took a mock bow while Pierre looked proudly on.

★ ★ ★

Pastor Paul telephoned while dinner was heating in the microwave — a deliciously baked chicken dish Gracie had frozen a week or so before, in expectation of her upcoming cooking crunch. Uncle Miltie replaced condiments and other ingredients used in the afternoon's baking — in two stages, carrying them in a basket as far as the stove, then positioning his walker so that he could reach all but the top shelf of each cupboard. At the sink, Marge and Pierre worked quite amicably over the mechanics of salad-making until Pierre — who had long since abandoned his fake accent — insisted on adding chopped boiled eggs, and Marge voiced her skepticism.

"I was just over to the church," Pastor Paul said, "and thought you'd want to know. The music stand's back."

Gracie's heart sank. "I was hoping —"

"Oh, the new one's still there." He whistled under his breath. "It's a beauty, isn't it? Seems we ought to refurbish the whole sanctuary just to provide an appropriate setting."

She laughed. "A good cleaning day would do wonders."

Marge and Pierre agreed to serve the salad in two bowls, one with eggs, the other without.

"Now the dressing . . ." Pierre insisted, and the battle was on again.

"What's going on there? Sounds like either a collaborative celebration or else World War Three."

"A little of each. Why don't you join us? It's only leftovers —"

"Your leftovers are better than most people's 'first-overs.' What time are we talking?"

"Imminently." The microwave signaled.

"I insist!" both Pierre and Marge said firmly. Simultaneously.

Pierre asked huffily, "Whose kitchen is this, anyway?"

"Gracie's!" Marge crowed.

"Not today!" Pierre sounded equally triumphant.

"Guess I'd better come," Pastor Paul chuckled. "You may need a chaplain to comfort the wounded."

"Please hurry. Casualties are mounting!"

As it happened, Rocky and Pastor Paul pulled in at the same time.

Gracie's first response was delight at seeing Rocky; her second, a fear that there'd never be enough food to satisfy those two gigantic appetites.

But of course, there would! The multigrain bread was bountiful and filling. And she could steal a bit from various containers intended for Saturday.

If all else failed, she still had the whole day tomorrow to make up any deficits.

Her heart sank. There was so much to do tomorrow! And efficiency would suffer if Pierre and Marge intended to defend every inch of culinary territory gained.

But where was her faith?

"Smells wonderful!" Pastor Paul inhaled, his expression ecstatic. Slowly cooked onions: irresistibly aromatic.

"No surprise, there." Rocky agreed.

"Eggs in the salad!" Pastor Paul said. "Wonderful!"

Pierre expanded.

Rocky made a face — though grinning — and Marge propped her fists with a "So there!" hmmmph.

"Pastor Paul," Gracie implored, "would you ask the blessing? Quickly, please!"

Once Pierre was delivered back to Pleasant Haven, Gracie suggested, "Let's stop by Cordelia's. See if Lacey's there."

Cordelia Fountain — outfitted in silk and lace, except for her Nikes — perched demurely on the porch swing, serving coffee from a silver service resting a bit unevenly on the ornate white wrought-iron table that usually graced her lawn. A couple in their fifties sat on the matching chairs. Knowing how heavy the furniture was, Gracie had to wonder how Cordelia had managed to get the three pieces onto the porch.

Perhaps — but not likely — Grif had helped her.

"Colonel and Mrs. Wilbert Vanderheim," Cordelia announced grandly, "Mrs. Gracie Lynn Parks and her uncle."

The man, blue eyes nearly disappearing in all the crevices arrowing from their corners, rose gallantly; the woman smiled, just barely, and nodded from behind her raised cup.

"George Morgan." Uncle Miltie braced on his walker and reached his hand. The men shook heartily, but Mrs. Vanderheim seemed to shrink into her chair at the possibility of physical contact.

Cordelia invited, "Do, please, join us."

Only lawn chairs were available. Gracie unfolded one for Uncle Miltie, then tried to find space for another. When there was none, she settled on the top porch step. No one but Uncle Miltie seemed to notice, and she silenced his concern with a smile.

"Mrs. Parks is one of Willow Bend's leading citizens," Miss Cordelia intoned, "and her uncle lives with her." Her voice

178

deepened. "Colonel Vanderheim is here on matters of great importance to our national defense."

When he laughed, his belly shook, Gracie noticed. She could like this man — even though chivalry might have demanded he at least *offer* her his chair!

"Scarcely that crucial," he said, "except to the chemical company I represent."

Warning signals sounded faintly in Gracie's brain. She looked for symptoms of out-and-out villainy and discovered none. Not on the surface, at least.

"They're planning on building between here and Mason City," Cordelia said, and added defiantly — perhaps because Uncle Miltie growled, deep in his throat — "It will mean hundreds of new jobs, possibly thousands!"

"I fear our dear hostess is given to exaggeration," the Colonel chuckled, "although I would hope our plant will make a change to this section of Indiana for many reasons, not the least of which is —"

"Pollution?" Uncle Miltie suggested. "Or do you refer to vandalizing a cemetery?"

Mrs. Vanderheim bristled and Cordelia sputtered, but the Colonel said affably, "That was what Mrs. Pomeroy feared. I was sent to address her concerns."

Cordelia said, with just the right amount of pathos, "It seems she owns some of the land his company needs, poor dear."

"And for which, I might add, we're willing to make a most generous offer! Unfortunately, we arrived to find the lady hospitalized." He took a sip of coffee, then said thoughtfully, "The daughter seems . . . uncertain." He set his cup down with a decisive rattle, which momentarily induced horror in Cordelia's expression. "And even if she were amenable to our offer — and if she had power of attorney, which, it seems, she does not — I would hesitate to take advantage of Mrs. Pomeroy in her unfortunate condition. Especially when she was so forthright in making her earlier objections known."

Mrs. Vanderheim made a sound that sounded suspiciously like a snort.

The Colonel's eyes crinkled again. "Perhaps you saw the papers. She dressed herself like some outlandish bird —"

"A loon, I believe," his wife sniffed. "*Quite* appropriate!"

"Now, dear. No, I think she meant to portray a swan, though her feathers were limp and dark. She flopped around gasping, croaking, 'Save me! Save me!' while others carried placards decorated with skull and crossbones and bearing the direst of warnings against us." He said with what seemed to Gracie like genuine respect, "When I meet a creative spirit such as hers, I fervently wish I could join her cause — whatever it may be!"

Gracie had been right the first time. She could, indeed, like this Colonel Vanderheim!

While they talked, Lacey came quietly around the house and settled herself in the tire swing. Planning to excuse herself, Gracie saw that she wouldn't be missed anyway — the topic had turned to baseball — and so she simply slipped away.

The child looked wan.

Gracie asked gently, "Is she no better, then?"

"Gram?"

Gracie hesitated. Who else would be of concern?

Lacey straightened. "Oh, Gram's better, at least a little. She squeezed my hand again, and tried to say my name, but I think her voice got rusty. And she liked the red flower I took." She sighed, "I was thinking . . . about someone else."

Gracie's heart ached. "Sometime, dear," she suggested, catching Lacey's hands in hers, "will you tell me about your mother? When you're not so tired," she added.

"It's not that I'm *tired* tired!" Lacey said with more spirit, "just tired of *him!* And her, sometimes. Mama would never have stayed with someone who treated her like that!"

Not for the first time, Gracie wondered, too, about Lacey's father . . . but this was not the time to ask.

"He treats her worse than . . . potato bugs!" She smiled. "Did I ever tell you 'bout how Gram paid me two cents apiece for potato bugs? Only she didn't want me to squash them. She said they're God's creatures, too — and we took them way, way out in the country, past all the farms — since we didn't want them to be on anyone else's potatoes, either — and we dumped them out deep in the woods. 'Let them eat skunk cabbage!' Gram said, and just laughed when I asked if the skunks mightn't be upset. Then she told me about some queen, long, long ago, who said something like that, only not about cabbage."

" 'Let them eat cake,' " Gracie quoted.

"Cake sounds a lot better than skunk cabbage!"

"Yes, even though it didn't mean cake like we have — just the messy stuff left over after bread-making, I believe."

"She must have been an evil queen — like in Snow White."

"Perhaps she was only thoughtless. Maybe she didn't understand."

Lacey nodded. "That's what Gram used to say about Aunt Kelly. That she just didn't understand." Her mouth tightened. "But Gram never said that about horrible old Uncle Grif!"

No, Gracie had to agree, if only in her thoughts. She suspected that Grif understood very, very well what he was about. And it alarmed her beyond belief that he worked at Pleasant Haven, where he could have easy access to Gillian Pomeroy. Could he, perhaps, already have done her harm? What if he were responsible, in some way, for her over-medication? *Thank You, Lord,* she thought quickly, *that now she's safe in the hospital.* Just then Lacey said, "You asked about Gram? They're sending her back to the home tomorrow."

Gracie had always made it a point to get plenty of sleep before a big catering event, but that night sleep seemed impossible. Her mind swirled with must-do's, although that was to be expected, and would, eventually, give in to weariness.

But these other concerns — Gram and Lacey . . . Kelly. . . .

Things didn't seem as simple as they

had earlier. Gillian Pomeroy's ownership of some of the land the chemical company required, coupled with her outspoken resistance to the project, made her a double threat. And even though Colonel Vanderheim was charming and — Gracie thought — sincere, he was only one in a company that might contain many who were not only insincere but unscrupulous. This latest development made it more difficult to settle on Grif as the villain, although, of course, he could be in collusion with someone else.

There was also the possibility that she was being an alarmist, that the over-medication had been an error, and that even now someone — realizing his or her honest mistake — was fearful of losing a job, or even of prosecution or lawsuit.

Lord, it's so much easier when there's clear-cut good and evil, black and white, no merging, or overlap. But it's so seldom that simple, is it? It wasn't for Your people even back in Bible times — not often was a situation as well-defined as the burning bush for Moses. For the most part those men and women floundered about, seeking Your will — or trying to avoid it — just as we do now.

There was so much more she wanted to put into words, but the capacity for expression seemed to abandon her. All she could come up with were fragments: Lacey, Gillian Pomeroy, Rocky, Pierre, Uncle Miltie, of course. . . .

If counting sheep induced sleep, why couldn't counting prayer requests do the same? Five times during the next ten minutes, she changed positions. Gooseberry had long since abandoned her and was snoring gently by the window.

It was nearly three when she gave up, dressed in her walking clothes and went downstairs. She yawned repeatedly as she washed potatoes for salad, then set out various Jello flavors and cans of fruit to be opened later. That done, she tried the couch for a nap, picked up a new mystery novel from the library and laid it down, and finally, with just the faintest tinge of dawn drawing a brilliant line along the horizon, she slipped a small flashlight and the house keys into her jacket pocket and set out for her earliest-ever praise walk.

She had gone more than a block before she realized that Gooseberry had slipped out with her.

"Where should we go, Gooseberry? You lead the way. Just no brambles and swamps, though, please."

His tail like a banner, flicking in and out

of her flashlight beam, he stalked ahead at a steady pace.

Gracie breathed deeply of that particular air characteristic of predawn — a mixture of mist, of dew-drenched grass — some newly mown — and then, as they reached the outskirts of town, a hint of woodsy scents. She caught the slightest flavor of skunk-spray, distant in time or place or both, and found it not at all unpleasant. *Lord,* she prayed, *perhaps Your Garden of Eden was much like this, though without pavement. I pray for those caught in big-city high-rises, in offices of glass and steel, or in institutions, where such experiences as this are unknown or, perhaps even worse, dimly remembered from some past time. It must be as hard for them as for the rich young ruler to get past the concrete and neon to a simple, heartfelt relationship with You.*

Startled, she stopped, turning off her flashlight both to save the battery and to focus her thinking. Who was she to set limits on humanity's universal yearning for their Creator, or on God's generous reaching-out to His children everywhere? She felt her face flushing. *Forgive me, Lord, for being smug and narrow. With You all things are possible, and concrete and steel are no barriers for You as You search and touch human hearts. Just because I feel closer to You when I walk through*

Your creation says more about me than about You and Your other children. She remembered her *Guideposts* magazines, always near her favorite resting chair or on her bedside table. No doubt they were published in a building of steel and glass and concrete; no doubt the editors and printers prayed as they manuevered through city traffic — just as she approached God in her praise-walks. And only look how many people were blessed by reading those articles of faith and miracle!

Lord, keep me from pride, she finished — for the moment — and was just about to switch on the flashlight when she heard a car approaching at a rate of speed too high for this narrow, winding stretch.

Common sense would dictate that she switch on the light to warn of her position. Certainly Gooseberry sensed foolishness in her stance. From a safe distance, he meowed warning. But while she did step from the berm into dew-wet grasses, something stayed her thumb on the switch.

Headlights bouncing, the car veered — more aimed, it seemed, than driven. Night was dimming just enough that Gracie could sense that it was a light color as it passed. The license plate, well-lit, was one of those vanity ones. It read VANDER 1.

Vander — Vanderheim — her heart sank. Had she been wrong, then, about the Colonel? Could any such pell-mell drive at this time of the morning not raise suspicion?

But suspicion of what?

Musing, she failed to recognize the approach of a second vehicle until, caught in the beam of its headlights, she realized she had stepped on the road again, her flashlight still unlit. Gooseberry's slight, furry body pressed on her ankles, trying to push her back to safety.

But the driver braked to a stop.

Thank You, Lord, she breathed. At least someone had his or her head together this morning.

She stepped closer to thank the driver. Gooseberry growled deep in his throat as a recognizable male voice snarled, "Well, if it ain't Miss Busybody herself. Too bad I didn't run you down." Grif Ransen grabbed her right hand, forced forward the flashlight switch and trained the beam upward — throwing his features into that malevolent mask teenage trick-or-treaters try to achieve. Grif was highly successful. Gracie tried to withdraw from his grasp but it only tightened, and he drew her so close that she could feel the heat and throb of the pickup's engine.

"Listen to me," he muttered, "and hear me good. You keep that nose of yours in the kitchen, or it'll be pointing straight up for good, six feet under. Got it?" He pushed her backward, gunned his engine and sped off.

She might have felt better if he had laughed. He didn't, and so she stood stunned, shivering, listening — half afraid he would decide to return and fulfill his grim promise. Finally, the brightening morning pressed its reassuring silence around her.

10

"Well, Gooseberry," she said, needing to hear a human voice, if only her own, "shall we continue?"

Gooseberry stretched and yawned — but he wasn't inattentive, she knew, to the sleepy birdsongs stirring the trees. Occasionally he paused to peer up, one front paw raised and his tail extended — for all the world like a hound-dog, pointing. Maybe Marge was right; maybe he and Charlotte both needed to see a good animal psychologist. But then they might feel duty-bound to chase one another, rather than continue to co-exist in such an unusual friendship.

"It's okay, Gooseberry. I love you even if you are, as Uncle Miltie says, a bubble off plumb." He peered over his furry shoulder at her — with tolerant affection, she thought.

They walked in companionable silence — she adjusting her earphones and humming along with a new gospel collection. It wasn't until Gooseberry stiffened at her side that her fear returned. There was another car coming behind them, and they stood less than midway on a one-lane bridge spanning a long, deep cut. Below them — far below — a tendril of Willow Creek rippled and giggled, scarcely more than a brook, now that the spring floods were long over. Even if she had wanted to jump the twenty or thirty feet between bridge and stream, she would first have to scramble onto a four-foot ledge of rough concrete.

Now what, Lord? She couldn't bring herself to turn, and wasn't that silly? Pretending that if she didn't see it — whatever *it* was — it couldn't be real, was a child's trick. Or an ostrich's.

The car was slowing, and — this had to be a good sign — Gooseberry had relaxed, was even purring as the vehicle stopped not far behind them.

Turning required every ounce of energy and courage she possessed.

"Gracie!" Rocky nearly tumbled from the driver's side. "What's wrong? You look —"

She felt herself sagging and welcomed his arms supporting her to the car.

"You've overdone," he scolded, and she had to smile — though tremulously — he sounded so much like El. "When are you going to learn to say 'no' to some of these unreasonable demands people make on you?"

A strange question, she thought, coming from the one who had arranged her next week's catering job.

He opened the passenger door and helped her in. "Don't you know how important you are — to everyone? To *me*, Gracie, if that means anything. What would I do without you stirring things up around here? Why, the *Mason County Gazette* would shrink by half!" Although she knew he was joking, his voice shook. It was time she set his mind at rest — on the one score, although that would certainly afflict him with new concerns.

She placed a hand on his arm. "Dear friend, I'm not worn out."

"No? You should see yourself! Pale, shaky — either you're worn to a nub or you've been frightened half out of your wits —"

She was nodding her head.

"Frightened? *You*, Gracie?" Now it was Rocky who looked as though he needed to sit down. *Rough, tough old Philadelphia newsman,* she thought fondly, *with a heart as hard as . . . Philadelphia cream cheese. . . .*

"Tell me," he demanded.

And she did, while Gooseberry renewed his surveillance of the flitting songbirds.

"I could kill him," Rocky said in a voice so matter-of-fact that she believed him.

"Rocky, he didn't hurt me, and he easily could have. Who would have known?"

"At least, now we take this to Herb."

"And he will do . . . exactly what?" She well knew that he and their police chief Herb Bower seldom saw eye to eye.

He shrugged. "He'll do something. He'll have to."

His jawline was set so grimly she was forced to revise her cream cheese assessment.

Chief Bower looked decidedly grim, too.

"He didn't hurt me," Gracie reiterated, "and he could have. Easily."

"That's not the point. He did lay hands on you and make threats." He made notations on a slip of paper and picked up the phone.

"You're bringing him in?" Rocky asked, apparently approving.

"Inviting him — very forcefully — to stop by."

"And if he doesn't?"

"*Then* I'll bring him in." To Gracie, he said, "Expect an apology before dinner."

As they left the office, Rocky asked, "Drop you off?"

She should walk, she knew, since her praise-walk had been abbreviated. But soon

Pierre, Marge and possibly Barb would be reporting for duty. "Please," she said.

Gooseberry, waiting by the car, scorned the offer of a lift. But then Gooseberry didn't have to make umpteen salads that day, as well as referee potential skirmishes.

Rocky drove the few blocks slowly, not speaking. *Worrying,* Gracie thought. She asked, "What were you doing out by Willow Run, anyway?"

"Had a hot tip," he said, grinning. "That old sow, Pigoletto, at the MacIvers had a record-breaking litter. I already sent Ben to shoot some color film."

He was whistling as he drove away.

Uncle Miltie was scrambling eggs. "You're up!" he said, his eyebrows escalating. "I was going to let you sleep late."

He may have forgotten what lay ahead of them today.

"Eggs?" he asked. "I added whipping cream, onions and paprika. You'll need all the boost you can get today."

So he hadn't forgotten. "Actually," she said, surprising herself, "yes, if you have enough for two."

"I'll make more." He shoveled an alarming heap to a plate, handed it to her, said, "Toast's in," and broke more eggs into a

194

bowl. "You must have beat the sun up today."

"Actually. . . ." But if she told him she hadn't slept at all, he'd fuss over her. She finished simply, "I was out rather early."

"See any deer?"

"Not a one." She poured two large glasses of ruby-red grapefruit juice.

"Any wildlife at all?"

That depended, she thought, but said, "Gooseberry and I smelled the aftermath of skunk."

"Sounds exciting." He added paprika in a red cloud.

"Exciting enough." She took a forkful of egg. "This is wonderful!" she said. "Have you ever thought of buying into a catering business?"

Pierre arrived first. Instead of a baseball cap, he wore a chef's hat with a fleur-de-lis on the side.

Uncle Miltie turned away, his shoulders shaking.

Blaise Bloomfield tapped on the door. "I know you must be overwhelmed . . . but sometime today, could you get away to check the setup near the arbor?"

"I'm certain that whatever you arrange —"

"Still, I'd feel better —"

"I'll call before I come," she promised.

"Calling won't be necessary." And just then Marge breezed in to rustle through the knife drawer for her favorite peeler.

It was going to be a long, long, long day.

And yet — by lunch break, the refrigerator was stacked with Bavarian creams, cheesecakes, and fruit Jellos. Already, vats of pasta, potato and macaroni salads had been taken to Marge's kitchen for storage. Wearing vinyl gloves — and his chef's toque askew, obscuring one eye — Pierre seemed content with creating canapes, while Marge stretched out on the couch, recovering from a chef-induced migraine.

It seemed almost criminal, when food was apparent everywhere, to serve her staff peanut butter sandwiches and apple slices, but Gracie knew that was all she had the space or energy to prepare.

Surveying the kitchen, Uncle Miltie suggested, "Let's eat outside."

Gracie found it a most delightful suggestion. They perched or sprawled on lawn chairs, plates balanced on their knees and cold drinks sitting precariously wherever they could find nearly flat surfaces. From his sun-worshipper's spot in the middle of the flower bed, Gooseberry ignored them —

sulking, Gracie knew. If they could banish him from a morning's activity, then he could very well do without them now. Charlotte — either more forgiving or less duplicitous — frolicked and posed, but even Marge seemed too tired to notice. Finally, Charlotte, too, found a nest among the flowers.

Marge held an ice-pack to her head.

Uncle Miltie snored lightly.

Leaf shadows moved scarcely at all. As Gracie crunched a section of crisp apple, Gooseberry glanced over, elevated his regal nose and yawned.

In contrast to this lethargy, Tish Ball and Tyne Anderson now walked briskly up the street, aprons over their arms and hair tucked up in turbans reminiscent of Carmen Miranda's. "We're ready and able, Gracie!" they chirped in unison. "Put us to work!"

Even Pierre groaned.

By 2:30, everything that could be ready was ready. Uncle Miltie still rested in his lawn chair, Gooseberry curled in his lap. Marge, not even checking her appearance in a mirror, left to walk the short distance to her house. The Turner twins, as fresh as ever, offered to clean up — and Gracie accepted with alacrity, lest they change their minds.

"Let's take you home, Pierre." Gracie dialed Blaise Bloomfield's number, found it busy and decided to go anyway. Blaise had, after all, said that a call wasn't necessary. "Pierre." She picked up her pocketbook.

"Before we leave," Pierre fished in his back pocket and extracted his billfold, "I must buy all rights to your recipe for Waldorf salad. I insist!"

Gracie was too tired to argue. "A million dollars?" she suggested.

He slapped a wad of Monopoly money onto the windowsill. "Done!" he said, doffing his white hat to the Turner twins.

Just as they were pulling out, Lacey came running, waving wildly. "Take me with you?" she asked, stopped to pant, then said, "Aunt Kelly didn't *tell* me to stay in the yard today!"

Blaise looked striking in watermarked silk, a matching scarf caught in a gold Celtic knot pin resting at mid-chest. As Fannie Mae heaved to a stop, she hurried from her office. "I've been watching, hoping —" She stepped back as Pierre and Lacey got out. "No one else —" she began, her smile fading.

"Pastor Paul seldom cooks," Gracie said, "and never for me."

Blaise blushed. "I didn't mean —" Then, placing her arm across Gracie's shoulders and heading toward the arbor she said, "But then we both know I did!"

Gracie chose to ignore the broad hint for a moment. "This is lovely! Perfect!" she raved, looking around. "You've arranged tables with plenty of room for serving —"

"Well, for wheelchairs and walkers, as well. Not many of our residents use them, but those who do need to be considered."

Gracie couldn't agree more. Often, she had seen Uncle Miltie try to squeeze through where even an unencumbered person would have to contort.

"You're bringing your own table coverings, I believe?"

Gracie nodded. "And if it rains?"

"It won't, of course." Blaise laughed lightly. "But there's Mason Hall. Is there anything else we can do for you at this point?"

"You've done marvelously. I couldn't ask anything more."

"Then let me ask something of you!" Blaise led her to a bench — the one where Gracie and Lacey had sat on their most recent visit.

Where was Lacey, anyway?

Blaise said, "We'll have a few minutes un-interrupted. I asked one of the attendants to take her to see her grandmother."

Gracie smiled, then stiffened. But no, of course not. Grif was in maintenance . . . and besides, Lacey wouldn't have gone with him without a fight.

"Now." Blaise smoothed her skirt over her knees. "Can we talk just a little about Pastor Paul? Personally, I mean."

Things have certainly changed from when I was a girl, Lord, she thought, more for herself than for Him. He'd noted the changes, she was certain. And had probably shaken His head over some of them. And even more since my mother's time. And Grandma! She had thought it was sinful to kiss before marriage . . . and even then, never in public. She thought it best not to remind Him how she and her friends had giggled over such prud-ishness. Now, here was a new century, and here was a very nice, proper-for-the-times young woman asking for information Gracie could supply, although not comfortably.

Blaise cleared her throat and smoothed her skirt over her knees. "Does he ever . . . talk about me?"

"Well, of course he does!" Gracie said, re-membering how he always mentioned her when he was picking up Pleasant Haven worshippers for church.

"But is it in a personal way, or —"

Even this new-century woman could blush. She leaned forward and asked earnestly, "Gracie, please be honest! Is there someone else in his life? Do you think there's possibly any chance for me? And will he be here, tomorrow?"

"He sings worse than he cooks. But I could ask him to do the prayer. How would that be?"

"Wonderful!" Blaise bounced a bit on the hard seat. "And is there . . . ?"

"Not that I know of. He keeps so busy with the church, with pastoral calls, with after-school activities for the children —"

Blaise waved that away. "I love all those things, too. I'll volunteer!" She waited.

Gracie said honestly, "Pastor Paul and I talk often, but I guess he knows more about my personal life than I do about his. He's a wonderful listener."

"He's a wonderful *everything!*" Blaise said raptly.

Smiling, Gracie knew that if he could see Blaise at this moment — starry-eyed, flushed, smiling — he would fall head over heels, if he hadn't already.

Any man would.

Gracie gave her a quick hug.

"Thank you." Blaise drew back, caught Gracie's hands in hers and squeezed. "And any unsolicited endorsements will be gratefully appreciated." She sighed. "Now let's go find Lacey for you."

Lacey was cuddled on the edge of Gillian Pomeroy's bed. When Gracie and Blaise entered, she scrambled off, but Blaise said, "It's all right, dear. I'm sure your grandmother appreciates your closeness."

Gillian Pomeroy lifted a hand — surely in assent — although her eyes remained closed.

"Did you see that, Gracie? Did you? She lifted her hand!"

Blinking tears, Gracie nodded.

Lacey was wriggling into a nest on the bed again.

Gillian must feel as though the Richter scale should register, Gracie thought — but the hand that had lifted reached out to rest on Lacey's knee.

"Ohhhhh!" Lacey laid both hands over it.

Blaise said softly, "I'll leave now. But you two stay as long as you like."

Lacey said, "I've been telling Gram stories about when she was young — like you suggested, Gracie. I know she hears me."

Giggling, she whispered, "I thought I might tell one wrong, on purpose, to see if she notices. You watch, too, Gracie — okay?"

Gracie promised.

"Anything at all. Like if she moves even a finger."

"I will."

Lacey burrowed into her nest. "Once upon a time," she began, "there was a little girl named Gram. She lived in a farmhouse near the Allegheny River in Pennsylvania. Her mother and father raised chickens, and it was her job, sometimes, to feed them. She particularly liked to go to the chicken house when there were little peeps keeping warm in the brooder. But there was one really nasty rooster that little Gram was afraid of. His name was Goliath." She whispered to Gracie, "So far it's true." She lowered her voice, speaking more intensely. "Little Gram's brother had gone to war. It was the Civil War, I think —" She waited, sighed and continued, "Yes, the *Civil War*, and he rode the family's best horse there."

There was no question. Gillian Pomeroy was reacting. Her head moved slightly sideways on the pillow. One hand flopped, as though agitated.

"See?" whispered Lacey. "She knows I'm wrong. Well maybe, then," she said in her "story" voice, "it was a bigger war, a world war, and her brother had gone to England."

Gillian seemed at peace once more.

"And wartime was a very bad time, so you couldn't get as much sugar as you needed for canning or Christmas candy. But a lot of funny things happened, too. One day, when it was wintry outside, little Gram was out rolling snowballs, and that big old nasty rooster came after her. He was shaking his head like a bull, that old red comb flopping, and little Gram didn't have a tree to climb or anything. So she took her biggest snowball and threw it just as hard as she could — *KA-WHOP!* And —" Lacey broke off, the breath apparently gone out of her, and Gracie heard it, too — a low, delighted chuckling. Gillian had not opened her eyes, but she was remembering the story. She gripped Lacey's hand, shaking it.

"I think she wants me to go on," Lacey said. "Don't you?"

There seemed no doubt of it.

"Well," she said, leaning even farther forward — until Gracie thought she might fall on her grandmother's face, "that old rooster stopped in mid-air, and squawked so loud little Gram thought for sure he'd eat her for dinner — and then he fell. Right down flat, his feathers all spread out over the snow and his beak wide open. And he lay there, not moving at all."

"And we. . . ." Gillian Pomeroy licked her cracked lips. "And we —" She shook Lacey's hand. Her eyelids fluttered, and for one wonderful moment her eyes were open and lucid.

"Oh, Gram!" Lacey was crying and laughing at the same moment. "Oh, Gram!"

"Lacey!"

Gillian Pomeroy started, then sighed, and her eyes drifted closed again, her hand falling away.

"Lacey, what are you trying to do?" Slapping an official-looking envelope onto the bedside table, Kelly dragged the child from the bed and shook her.

Gracie started to rise to Lacey's defense, but Grif Ransen blocked her way. Unwilling to make a scene in a hospital room, Gracie sat back down. But she was filled with indignation.

"Your mother was responding!" she pointed out. "Kelly — don't you *want* her well again? That can't be true!"

Kelly's face drained white. Releasing Lacey, she sank into a chair, breathing in small pants, while Lacey looked from Gracie to her aunt, her eyes clouded and her chin quivering.

"Don't listen to her," Grif said. "We know what we have to do, babe. Don't go soft on me now."

Kelly drew a shuddering breath, then straightened and said coldly, "Lacey, go home and stay in your room until I — we — get back. And you, Mrs. Parks, I can't have you upsetting my mother any longer." She met Gracie's glance directly. "If you interfere again, I'll have to — to go to the police."

Grif stepped out of Gracie's way. "That reminds me," he said, "Bowers said I had to apologize to you. Consider it done — not that much is changed. Guess I can't get away with running *you* down. But nobody cares about a stupid orange cat. Right?"

"Gracie. Gracie —" Lacey tugged at Gracie's hand as they moved along the corridor. "He meant Gooseberry, didn't he? He means he's going to hurt Gooseberry —" Her voice faded to a sob.

But Gracie had more immediate concerns. He — and Kelly, who seemed to move at Grif's will like a marionette — were at that very moment alone with Gillian Pomeroy. And that did not bode well for the helpless woman.

No one seemed to be on duty at the infirmary office, but in a narrow side room a young woman in a pale blue uniform pulled files from a high shelf.

"Miss —"

The files showered down, a flurry of manila folders and multi-colored forms. Shrugging, the young woman stepped over them. "It's been that kind of day. Meg's on break. How can I help —" She broke off, frowning. "What's wrong?" she asked tensely.

"Mrs. Pomeroy. I believe she may be in great danger."

"But her daughter's with her now. She came in just a bit ago. If there's a problem, why hasn't she —"

Gracie drew a deep breath. *Am I wrong on this, Lord? Could I have misinterpreted? But what if I'm not wrong, and say nothing* — "I believe," she said, "that her daughter *is* the danger. Or at least a part of it."

The young woman touched a button and spoke into a receiver. "Will an attendant please report to Room 103. *Stat.*" Breaking the connection, she said, "We can't take a chance, can we — just in case."

"Do I *have* to go home?" Lacey asked, as Gracie steered Fannie Mae out of the parking lot. "Can't I stay with you?" She straightened. "I could protect Gooseberry from Uncle Grif!"

Gracie manuevered the curving exit before answering — and then with a question. "Lacey, has your aunt ever . . . hurt you?"

Lacey shrugged. "Aunt Kelly's not a bad person. She yells at me — lots — but she's never really, really hurt me." She added thoughtfully, "And I don't think she'd ever let Uncle Grif hurt me, either."

"Then I have to take you home."

"I knew you'd say that. I guess if you don't, they might come and hurt Gooseberry."

"Oh, no, dear child! That's not the reason. It's because Aunt Kelly is your legal guardian. I have no right to go against her wishes." Unless you were in danger, she added in her thoughts, and then I wouldn't give you up even if Herb Bower dragged me away in chains.

She couldn't help smiling at that unlikely prospect.

But it brought another thought to mind. She really should stop by the police station again, just let Herb know these current concerns — not that there was much he could do about it, unless real harm did come to Gillian Pomeroy. And in that case, it might well be too late.

★ ★ ★

Herb leaned back, a sweating can of soda in his hand, his feet on his desk.

"Don't," she said, when he moved to straighten. "You don't have to look official for friends."

"Want something to drink?"

She sank onto a padded straight chair. "Just a friendly ear."

"You're in luck! I have two." When minutes passed and she said nothing further, he lowered his feet and leaned forward. "Spit it out, Gracie. It's that Grif Ransen again, isn't it?"

"I'm concerned about Mrs. Pomeroy." She related the afternoon's events.

He crumpled the can and tossed it to a recycling bin. The lid swung, and the can rattled in. "Two points," he grinned. "Gracie, there's so little I can do."

"I know."

"But you were right to tell me. And you were right to alert the officials there, too. He'd be stupid to try anything with them watching." He sighed. "Whatever possessed them to hire that guy? One look, and you see he belongs on a mug shot." He stroked his chin. "What is it you suppose he wants, anyway? Money's the first thing that comes to mind. But does she have any? She was always involved in protests and causes — that tends to drain the resources. Her insurance must be paying for the convalescent time at Pleasant Haven."

Gracie said thoughtfully, "Unless it's *potential* wealth —" and suddenly, as though she were reliving the moment, she remembered Colonel Vanderheim, mentioning that a piece of land crucial to his chemical company's expansion belonged to Gillian Pomeroy.

"She'd *never* sell!" she said, rising out of the chair. "She'd been picketing against the plant since it was first mentioned!"

"What plant?"

"And the Colonel said that Kelly doesn't have power of attorney!"

"What Colonel?" Herb asked.

"And he said that, anyway, he wouldn't want the land against her wishes. He'd hoped to convince her."

Herb leaned back again, hands laced behind his head. "I'm sure you'll tell me when you're ready," he said mildly.

"And there was that official-looking envelope —" She slapped her hand on his desk. "That's it, Herb!"

He only smiled.

"They're trying to get her to sign over power of attorney! Just keeping her doped up enough that they won't have any trouble exercising it! You should have seen them when she was coming around. I don't think they really want to kill her — well, at least her daughter doesn't. But they came close that one time. And they could again . . . unless we stop them."

"Can't find anything in here," Uncle Miltie grumbled to himself, as he peered into the refrigerator. "Leastways, nothing we're allowed to eat."

Gracie smiled. "Just as the shoemaker's children go barefoot, the caterer's uncle goes hungry."

"And her cat." Uncle Miltie peered over his shoulder. "Didn't hear you come in, Gracie." The refrigerator door shushed shut. "How about I take you out to eat tonight? Wouldn't think you'd want to look another stove burner in the eye."

"And it would be nice to get away." A strange thing to say, she thought, when she'd been away for the past few hours. "Away from kitchen things — anything we'd have to clean up."

I'm so blessed, Lord, in all these friends. What would I do without them? She thought of Gillian Pomeroy. *She needs a friend, Lord. I know she has You. And she may have* dozens back in Mason City, but for whatever reason they're not here now. Lacey loves her, but she's just a child and can't help much. I think she needs me. Not just me, but that could be a start. Herb's watching, too — but that Grif's a sly one, and he seems determined — and I'm not sure he cares enough even about Kelly that he'd let her get in the way. Help us to keep a sharp lookout, will You? Help us to keep her safe. And Lacey, too. Amen.

"What'd He have to say?" Uncle Miltie asked, grinning.

Gracie glanced up.

Uncle Miltie patted her arm. "You think I don't know when you're talking to God? Put in a good word once in a while for me, too, girl — okay?"

"I always do," she said, just as the phone rang.

"Get that, Gooseberry!" Uncle Miltie called as he struggled with his walker.

But Gracie reached it easily, and was glad when she heard Rocky's voice.

"I've been worried about you all day," he said. "Especially when I stopped by and Miltie said you weren't there. I pictured you out walking deserted roads again."

"But if I were there —"

"I know, they wouldn't be deserted." He growled, "You've been listening to Uncle

Miltie's logic for too long."

"I was checking out the set-up for to-morrow."

"I heard."

"You . . . heard?"

"Called Herb, to see if he'd talked to Ransen again." Silence vibrated over the wire. "Gracie —"

She waited.

"I want you to promise me something."

She continued to wait.

"No more walks until this is settled."

"Rocky!"

"I want you to give your word. Otherwise, the dogs and I will accompany you every morning."

"Promise?" she asked lightly.

"Don't be coy. Those mutts would give Gooseberry cardiac arrest, and you know it."

"How was Pigoletto?" she asked. "Maternity agreeing with her?"

"Don't change the subject."

"I won't promise, Rocky — not for anyone. I won't be a prisoner. Tomorrow, I'll be too busy anyway. But Sunday I fully intend —"

"Afternoon, though. I'll go with you."

"But you can't Monday. Or Tuesday. Or —"

"We'll discuss it."

"I thought that's what we *were* doing."

"Let me take you out for a bite to eat. Now."

"I already had an offer —"

"Uncle Miltie?"

"You're so certain no one else would ask me —"

"Wish I were!" he said lightly. "But attractive women like you don't come along all that often."

At least he was in a joking mood again.

"I'll pick you both up. In about fifteen minutes?"

"That's lovely of you. We'll be ready and waiting."

Gracie now had two dates and not a single certainty that she knew what to do next.

11

If weather were any indication, Pleasant Haven's Family Day would be an unqualified success.

Gracie had set her alarm for four, and Gooseberry — apparently anticipating another early walk — padded to the kitchen door and waited. "Not today," she told him. She didn't know quite how to explain to him that he wouldn't be free to ramble during the day until the Grif Ransen problem was solved.

She did let him out — "Just for a few minutes, you hear —" and stayed close to the door to wait for him.

Breathing deeply of the predawn fragrances, she prayed. *Thank You, Lord. And keep us calm and efficient during this day — keeping in mind that our main goal is to serve these senior citizens and their families. Let us not lose patience with any guest — or with ourselves. Amen.*

There. That felt better.

Not too happy about it, Gooseberry nevertheless came back in at her first call. She turned the oven on to preheat, retrieved the trays of stuffed chicken breasts and salisbury steaks from the freezer, and sat down to check her list of "things to do" before setting off for Pleasant Haven.

When dawn arrived, it came softly in pinks and lavenders touched with gold. She watched raptly as silhouetted trees and shrubs gained shape and texture, as sleeping homes came to life, one light at a time . . . as pearlized shades of blue dominated the sky. *Such a wonderful world, Lord . . . How can anyone argue that this all happened by accident?*

"Only nine o'clock — and I think we're ready." Gracie checked her list one more time, scanned the kitchen to see if anything still waited for packing, and smiled.

"Good help makes all the difference!" Uncle Miltie said.

"Modest, as always."

"Truthful, in any event."

She was about to agree when the front doorbell rang.

"Back in a minute," she said, hoping it wasn't someone who'd involve her in a long conversation. Maybe Marge, saying she needed help with loading her van. But

Marge never went to the front door, just came in the back, usually without warning.

"The Morgan house?" a young male voice asked.

"Ye-es." The local flower shop's car stood in the driveway.

"Sign, please, Mrs. Morgan?"

She didn't bother to correct him. He was a teenager she didn't know.

He looked at her signature. "Gracie Lynn. . . ."

"Parks," she said.

"I . . . see."

"George Morgan is my uncle."

"Um hmm." He produced a huge bouquet of snapdragons.

Propping the door open with one elbow, she managed to crowd them inside. "Thank you."

"Don't mention it."

Uncle Miltie thumped his walker close. "Someone has an admirer!"

"Indeed, someone does." She chuckled.

"Not from Rocky?"

"Not for me at all."

"Gooseberry, then." He fumbled for a card.

"This is no time to turn modest." She struggled to contain the bundle until they reached the living-room table. "Well?"

He handed her the card. It read, "Sweet, but with swagger — like you!" and it was signed, "A Secret Admirer."

"It *must* be for you, Gracie!"

"The name he gave was *Morgan*."

He scratched his head. "But —"

"Don't fight it," she urged. "Your irresistible charms are something you'll have to bear, like it or not."

"Should I get a vase?" he grumbled, "or just dump them now." But he was already on his way, whistling.

Just as they were ready to leave for Pleasant Haven, the doorbell rang again. Marge had already driven off in the fully loaded van.

"What now?" Gracie sighed.

"Maybe they're back for the snapdragons. Realize they made a mistake."

But it was Lacey who stood there, wearing a frilly dress. She turned for inspection. "Is this okay?"

"You look beautiful, but your aunt said —"

Lacey shrugged. "She . . . was okay this morning."

"She said you can go? With me?"

Lacey looked out from under her lashes. "She didn't say I couldn't."

"What, exactly, did she say?"

"She didn't say anything."

"Ah."

"I knew she was leaving for somewhere, so I just pretended I was still asleep, even when she came over and spoke my name. 'Lacey. Lacey.' That's how she said it, Gracie, softly, like she didn't hate me at all. She really, truly can be very, very nice."

Gracie hugged the child.

Lacey said firmly, "If you don't take me with you, I'll walk. And with these shoes, I'd get blisters." While she didn't add, "and it will be all your fault," Gracie got the message.

"You know I'll have to try to call her, just to be certain."

"Sure. But she won't be there." She tugged on Gracie's hand, drawing her back momentarily. "Nobody has a right not to let me sing for God, Gracie!" When Gracie offered no rebuke, she asked confidently, "Why don't I just go sit in the car with Uncle Miltie?"

Gracie held the receiver while the dial tone buzzed and Lacey's words repeated themselves through her mind. She was right, of course. No one had authority to deny another soul expression of its love for God. *Lord, am I doing the right thing?*

Dialing, she knew that she had to try, at least.

Three rings. Four. Five. She was just about to hang up when an expressionless voice answered, "Yes?"

"It's . . . Gracie Parks."

A pause. Then, "Is Lacey with you?"

"Yes. She wants —"

"Take her. I know how important today is to her. I went to her room to tell her when — when I had to leave for a while, but she was asleep. Mrs. Parks —"

Gracie waited, then asked, "Yes?"

"I'm not a monster, Mrs. Parks. I love my mother and my niece. It's just —"

When she didn't continue, when Gracie heard the unmistakable sounds of swallowing and sniffling, Gracie said, "I think I understand, dear. And my prayers are with you."

"But I don't see —" She was sobbing, then.

"Why don't we talk over a cup of tea? Perhaps even this evening."

"I . . . yes," Kelly finished softly, her voice trembling. "Thank you."

Lacey and Uncle Miltie were waiting for her in Fannie Mae. Not looking up, the little girl said, "I told you she wouldn't be there."

Gracie inserted the key in the ignition. "She was."

Lacey stiffened. "But you're letting me go anyway?"

"*She's* letting you go! That's what she wanted to tell you this morning. And . . . she sends her love." *That's nearly the truth,* she told herself and God. *It was at least implied.*

"I can't believe it!" Lacey replied, then quickly amended, "I told you she's not a bad person! I'll bet God changed her mind. Don't you think?"

Did You? Gracie thought. *I wouldn't be the least surprised!*

Blaise Bloomfield looked radiant in a crisp linen shirtwaist and a wide leather belt. Both hands extended, she came to greet Gracie. "Is he? Will he?" Her eyes were as bright as her shiny silver earrings.

Gracie nodded.

"You must think I'm acting like a teenager."

Gracie grinned. "On you, it looks good."

"When, then?"

"I told him we'd plan to eat at twelve. He'll be here before that."

"Wonderful."

"We're keeping a very close watch on Mrs. Pomeroy," she added. Actually, she told them, Gillian Pomeroy was resting quite comfortably this morning. Her sleep had seemed natural, the night supervisor thought. Once she stirred, and it seemed she might be waking.

Blaise turned in a swirl of skirt to stoop to Lacey's height. "And how are you today? How lovely you look! Would you like to help me with streamers? And later — we'll be having some games for the children. I'd be delighted if you'd be my assistant!"

While Lacey flitted here and there, bubbling and glowing, Gracie and Uncle Miltie set centerpieces and placemats. The Turner twins — in matching fluffy white aprons and waltz-length blue-checked skirts — and Marge — wearing an animal print, its colors as wild as the beasts it depicted — were already hard at work.

Suddenly, Pastor Paul appeared, looking expectant.

Gracie glanced to see if Blaise had noticed.

Ah, yes!

"Why are you grinning?" Uncle Miltie asked suspiciously, then watched Blaise's movement toward the object of her affection.

By 10:30, there was no time for ruminating about dreaming hearts. The choir —

minus only those few who had given notice they couldn't attend — had arrived, and Barb, at the keyboard, was running them through their warm-up scales. She insisted that Gracie join them.

"We need your alto for balance!"

But Gracie knew that it was really a ploy to help keep the Turner twins on pitch.

Leaving her grandmother napping in her wheelchair, Lacey took her place near Estelle. True to Blaise's word, Gillian Pomeroy was not left unattended. Although the young woman attendant seemed engrossed in an inspirational romance novel, she was close by and looked up often. No one else seemed interested in the two women in the shady area. Gracie noted with deep relief that Grif Ransen, in particular, was nowhere in view.

"Now," Barb suggested, "let's run through 'Morning Has Broken'." Her voice took on an edge of panic. "Where are you going now, Gracie?"

"I'll sing from where I'm working," Gracie promised. This was one of those days when a split personality was definitely called for. While Barb tested the early phrases of each song they planned to perform, Gracie lifted lids, adjusted heat and tried to suppress the flutters of tension that never failed to show themselves at this stage of preparation.

It seems ridiculous, Lord, for me to have butterflies. I've done this hundreds of times and should realize that all the little quirks and wrinkles work themselves out.

But then she remembered the celebrated opera singer who insisted that when he wasn't nervous before a performance, he knew that he wouldn't do well: he required that edge of tension to produce his best work.

And while it isn't exactly an aria, Lord, this day is *important to a lot of people.* She paused to look around the grounds, filling with family and staff. As soon as Barb released the choir, Lacey perched near her grandmother. She seemed to be singing softly while she held the limp hand. *Please, Lord, could Gillian Pomeroy wake up today? Really communicate with that dear child — even if only for a few minutes?*

"Mrs. Parks," Blaise was saying, leading an entourage towards her. "Let me introduce you to a few members of Pleasant Haven's board of directors."

Eudora McAdoo soon made her appearance. Gracie paused in her current task of measuring coffee into the largest urn to note that the woman's hair now bore a turquoise tint, matching her necklace, bracelet and the mammoth daisies of her swirly dress.

Marge paused to whisper, "I wonder if she paints her toenails to match?" Her voice held more awe than ridicule.

Uncle Miltie soon clumped over, his expression stormy. "Can't you find a job for that bothersome woman to do?"

Gracie couldn't help herself. She teased, "I believe turquoise is just your color."

He glared. "Remind me, please, Gracie Lynn Parks, to write you out of my will!"

"As soon as we get home," she said sweetly, and went to help Marge.

"You're evil," Marge said in a tone that indicated her approval. "Poor Uncle Miltie."

"He is having a bad day, poor dear," and she told about the snapdragons.

They both watched Eudora McAdoo, chatting with a bevy of friends, at the same time keeping an eagle eye out for Uncle Miltie's whereabouts.

Marge asked seriously, "Doesn't that qualify as stalking?"

"I doubt if Herb would find sufficient threat. Oops. There's Barb, beckoning."

"Splendid!" Blaise's praise for the proceedings pleased Gracie as she replenished drinks at the table where Pastor Paul sat with the dignitaries, and — Gracie was amused to note — Pierre and his frequent attendant. "Everything is simply perfect!"

"Pierre deserves a great deal of credit," Gracie said, pouring decaf.

"Bravo!" Uncle Miltie, standing nearby, had overheard and chose to offer a salute. Gracie repeated the cheer softly. "Bravo, Chef Pierre!" Pierre nearly upset the table as he stood to bow for his admirers.

"You know, I'd love to have him help occasionally," Gracie said. "But what about right here, as well, in the kitchen?"

"The food could certainly use the help!" Uncle Miltie contributed. "I remember those cookies!" He shuddered.

Blaise looked thoughtful.

While tables were cleared for dessert, the choir sang again. "Go along." Uncle Miltie shooed Marge, Gracie and the Turner twins aside. "Paul and I can manage here."

"I'll be happy to help," Blaise offered. "Paul, you and I could take that half, and —"

"I'll help George!" Eudora McAdoo purred.

Gracie said, "But you should be with us — in the choir."

She was poised to refuse, until Estelle suggested, "Eudora, dear, perhaps you shouldn't — when you've been to only the *one* practice." That was all it took.

Eudora tossed her head and followed Gracie, while Uncle Miltie wiped his forehead on a crumpled napkin and Estelle sniffed.

Because Lacey's voice — for all its beauty — was light, Barb had suggested she sing a solo following dessert. The child was fidgeting, her mouth small and eyes huge. Gracie threw her a warm smile, but Lacey just mouthed the words, "I'm scared."

"I have an idea," Gracie told her. "Think about ice cream."

"Ice cream?" Lacey licked her lips happily, in anticipation.

"*After* you sing."

"Oh, yeah. Barb says no milk or chocolate. Why is that?"

"I'm not certain. Coats your throat, or something. But right now — why don't you go talk to your grandmother for a few minutes? You could even take her some dessert."

"She'd like that!" She accepted the dish and spoon and was off in a flash of ponytails.

Smiling, Gracie watched. Gillian Pomeroy truly was improving, now that she was being so closely observed and her medication carefully monitored.

Lacey waved, making a thumbs-up sign, and Gracie saw with pleasure how Gillian had accepted the dish into her own hands, and while she fumbled with the spoon, was trying. *Thank You, Lord! Thank you! Thank you!*

"Have you seen Lacey?" Barb asked. "Don't you think it's time we have her sing? I've noticed a few people getting restless."

Lacey turned, just then, kissed her grandmother's cheek and handed the dish and spoon to the young attendant. She ran back to Gracie and hugged her. "I'm not as afraid as I was," she whispered. "Seeing Gram better makes me want, more than anything, to sing for her. As if no one else was here."

Gracie nodded, and immediately prayed for both of these new friends. A little girl who sang like an angel was an angel of love to her grandmother. And what could be more appropriate for a day consecrated to celebrating families?

Barb hit the opening notes, but people continued to talk and eat. Lacey was so short that no one saw her, standing stiff and ready.

"Here." Gracie's minister had pulled a chair beside the chord organ and helped Lacey up. "Do you want me to steady you?" he asked.

"I'll be —" She cleared her throat. "Fine."

Please, Lord. Gracie was trying a bit of angel duty herself.

Still the room was noisy.

Barb struck a loud chord, as Paul used his most impressive pulpit voice to announce, "And now, Miss Lacey Carpenter will favor us with a solo — her first ever."

There was a spattering of applause, then expectant silence. Gracie glanced toward the shady spot where Gillian Pomeroy sat. Mrs. Pomeroy leaned forward, hands clasped.

Her attendant carried the dish to a sideboard and sat on a bench, her attention also on Lacey.

The girl's first notes wavered a bit, and Pastor Paul reached to touch her arm, as though to steady her on her perch.

". . . in His hands," Lacey sang, her own small arms open.

Her voice was as sweet as a spring morning. Gracie closed her eyes to absorb its clarity, the miracle of its promise. *Dear Lord, thank You for blessing her — and us — with such beauty. And that Your gift to her is returned to You so worshipfully —*

Lacey was approaching the final phrase, when suddenly she broke off with a gasp. Gracie looked up to see her face draining of color as she tumbled from the chair before

Pastor Paul could either assist or catch her. The chair fell backward, crashing against the keyboard, producing an alarmed dissonance.

"Gram!" Lacey was shrieking as she raced among the tables. "Gram! Gram! Where are you?"

12

Gracie stared at the empty spot where Gillian Pomeroy's wheelchair had rested. Gillian's assigned attendant was turning from one side to another, her expression distraught. As Gracie strode towards her, she could see her distress escalating. "Help! Come help!" she shouted.

Poor thing. She had relaxed her diligence for just those moments when Lacey sang. Whoever had spirited Lacey's grandmother away must have been waiting for just such an opportunity. And now that poor young woman was left with the guilt.

Moving swiftly, Gracie caught the child close, attempting the soothing phrases that come naturally to a mother. "There, there, there, dear. It's going to be all right."

But *was* it? Her instincts told her that Gillian Pomeroy must be found soon if she were to be found safe. She couldn't be far away. Had Herb been called? "Wait here, just a bit." She led Lacey to a bench — the bench she and Amy had used when they had first met Lacey and her grandmother.

Uncle Miltie spoke from beside her. "Do what you need to, Gracie. I'll stay with her."

Nodding, Gracie hurried to find Blaise. "Has anyone called Herb Bowers?"

"Nine one one," Blaise answered. "Of course. But how could this have happened?"

"How many exits are there?"

"Exits?"

"From the grounds," Gracie explained. "How many ways someone could take if —"

She heard sirens. *Thank You!*

"Two," Blaise said dully. "Two exits."

Pierre's young attendant was at her shoulder. *Timothy,* his name-tag read. Why had Gracie never noticed that before?

Timothy said, "I'll search the infirmary."

"Search . . ." Blaise murmured. "Good idea."

Strange, Gracie thought, *how someone can be so confident and efficient in some areas, and so useless in others.* She urged Blaise to a chair. "Why don't you sit down, dear? I know it's a shock. You need to get a calm breath."

Blaise did not even look up when Pastor Paul said urgently, "Gracie, tell me what to do."

"Herb's here." A police car was just then maneuvering the winding driveway. "Could you fill him in? And tell him there's another exit."

"Two exits," Blaise repeated. She was pale but starting to look more like her own capable self.

Timothy was back. "The infirmary's clean. Two of the guys are checking the rest of the building — and somebody else will make the rounds of the residences and Mason Hall. The police are here, I see. What next?"

"What outbuildings are there?" Gracie asked.

"A storage barn — for outdoor furniture in the winter months. Other stuff, too. Maintenance shed — tractors, mowers, all kinds of equipment."

Gracie started. Could it be . . . ? If Grif were involved in this — and every atom of her mind shrieked that he must be — where could he feel more secure than in the maintenance shed?

"Go with you?" Timothy asked.

Gracie hesitated. He would certainly know the area. But — "If you tell me what I'm looking for —"

"Dark red, white trim. It's marked."

"Then — could you send the police there?"

Moving at a run, Herb Bower was approaching from the parking lot. She didn't wait; he'd catch up long before she herself reached the maintenance shed.

This was not a shed, Gracie decided — it was too big. But the sign told her she was at the right place. There were few windows in the building, and those very small, but several skylights broke the line of the ridged metal roof. A wide entranceway stood partially open.

They're there, aren't they, Lord? Nowhere else would make sense.

Of course, this made little sense anyway. While Grif might have thought the large gathering would make it easier to slip his victim out of sight without detection — as indeed it had — that same number made it nearly impossible for him to get away with her.

Unless they were already off the grounds.

Or unless all he really wanted, at least for now, was to force Gillian to sign a power of attorney. Yet as strong-willed as the woman had always been, Gracie knew she must have some resistance left in her. Besides, what use would a power of attorney document be to Grif Ransen — or to anyone — if Gillian were left in a condition where she could make her own decisions? New fear cramped Gracie's breathing. She had to hurry!

All of a sudden, she felt a touch at her shoulder and a tug at her apron. Lacey, breathing hard, stood there. "Uncle Miltie didn't want me to come. But I have to. *You* understand, don't you, Gracie?"

Gracie squeezed her hand in answer. They were drawing close, and she didn't want to alert anyone inside the maintenance structure. Lacey put an index finger to her lips and began to tiptoe. Gracie had to smile. *What a blessed child, Lord — and what love she has for her grandmother! Please help us to find Gillian Pomeroy safe and sound.*

Nonetheless, if she should be neither safe nor sound, it was important that Lacey not be one of the first to know.

Gracie pulled the child to her and spoke in a whisper. "Stay out here, dear, just until we find her." When she began to protest, Gracie added, "You wouldn't want to make it more difficult for anyone, would you? The police will be worried about you, and unable to give their whole attention to your grandmother."

Quickly, Lacey drew back, pressing close against the building. "Call me, right away?"

Gracie nodded. Herb, as she had hoped, now appeared.

Together they entered the building, its interior dark in contrast to the sun they had just left.

A disadvantage, Gracie knew, if anyone already inside happened to be watching. Instinctively, she moved into deeper shadow until her eyes could adjust.

It was still, except for those noises any building makes when inhabitants remain quiet — tickings, creakings, something that might be a mouse chewing, though Gracie wondered what among the mowers and heavy equipment, shelves of tools and barrels of paint and oil even the least discriminating mouse might find appetizing.

Herb indicated that she should remain where she was, so she moved only to a slatted wall divider where she could watch. She knelt on a crate, next to one half-open and filled with uneven chunks of metal, apparently broken machine parts. Herb moved with a sure confidence and quiet tread, staying near the wall. He was avoiding those areas of floor spotlighted from the skylights Gracie had noticed earlier.

Soon he was back. "Nothing obvious," he said quietly, "though the office door seems to be locked. I'll check the storage barn, see if they're there, then come back. You'd best wait. They might still bring her here when they think the coast is clear."

"Then send Lacey in, will you?" She wouldn't want the child outside alone, in that event. "We'll stay hidden," she assured him.

Lacey slipped in, blinking. "It's so dark here!"

"Your eyes become accustomed to it more quickly than you think."

Lacey perched on a smaller box. "If Gram's not here, where is she?" Her lip trembled.

Gracie reached to hug her. "I wish I knew."

For long moments, they sat in the still ominous silence. Both shifted their positions, looked at one another, then sighed.

Suddenly, a sharp rasping sound shattered the stillness. Lacey looked up with startled eyes. Gracie, aware of a new, quieter sound — a whirring — touched her lips. Surely, wheels moving — carefully, stealthily, pausing often as though someone listened.

But who? Someone, apparently, who had eluded Herb's search. Where? In the locked office? Would that explain the sharp, rending sound?

Lacey seemed to be holding her breath. Gracie crept, inch by inch, along the slatted wall. She could see little past the jumble of machinery, only a bit of muted color that might be clothing, or paint-rags, or no fabric at all.

More daring than Gracie, as well as smaller, Lacey slipped to a spot uncontained by the wall. Suddenly, she sprang forward, arms waving. "Gram!" she called. "Oh, *Gram!*"

Throat clogged, pulse pounding, Gracie followed in time to see Lacey catapult her small frame against her grandmother and her wheelchair. It was Gillian who broke the entanglement. She pressed fingertips against her throat, as though to facilitate speech. "They were . . . here." She cleared her throat. "Gone, now."

"They?"

Massaging her throat again, Gillian sighed.

"We'll help, Gram," offered Lacey. "We'll ask questions. You just nod or shake your head. Was Uncle Grif here?"

A nod.

"Aunt Kelly?"

Gillian shook her head.

"*Not* Aunt Kelly?

"No."

"But you said 'they.' Who else?"

Gracie suggested, "It might not matter now. Mrs. Pomeroy, did they bring you here?"

Again, her head shook in negation.

Lacey protested, "But they must have!"

"Unless," Gracie had an inspiration, "you came here yourself? You knew they would look for you — and you beat them to it?" Each question was followed by a nod.

Lacey said, "Oh, Gram! You're so . . . brave!"

Gillian Pomeroy smiled, eyes twinkling.

Gracie continued, "But they did come looking for you? And you hid."

Two nods answered.

"In the office?"

That nod had barely begun when Grif Ransen's harsh voice said triumphantly — "And this time we found you! Didn't we?"

Lacey shrank against Gracie. Gillian leaned back in her chair, her eyes blazing and chin firm. Gracie turned to see who the other part of the "we" was. She would have been prepared for a timid Kelly, or for another man, but she would never in a hundred years have expected Mrs. Vanderheim, looking not in the least genteel.

Grif swaggered to the outer door, shutting and bolting it, testing to be certain it was secure. "We should have known Mrs. Nosey Lynn Parks would be in on this somewhere." He approached Gracie with a purposeful stride. "Remember what I promised you, that day on the road?"

"You will *not* hurt Gooseberry!" Lacey

flared, drawing much of her courage, it seemed, from her tight clutch on Gracie's apron.

I forgot to take off my apron, Lord! she thought in surprise. *Now, wasn't that foolish?*

Although perhaps not as foolish as being caught in this situation with Grif and his unexpected cohort.

"Gooseberry?" Grif hooted. "That ratty orange cat?"

"He's not ratty!"

"Shut up, kid, or you'll be sorry. And you don't have no nine lives."

Gracie shushed the child with pats.

"Smart lady," Grif grunted. To Gillian, he said, "All we want from you is your signature."

Gillian Pomeroy clenched both lips and hands.

"Oh, you'll sign, all right." He made a grab for Lacey, but Gracie pushed the child behind her.

Mrs. Vanderheim said in a reasonable voice, "We don't want anyone to get hurt here." The coldness in her eyes — and Grif's snort — belied her gentle words. But she herself, Gracie thought, would want no actual part in any mayhem.

Gillian pressed a hand to her throat in a

gesture Gracie was finding familiar. "Kelly," she said, her voice grating.

Grif sneered. "If she had half the starch you have, old lady —"

Mrs. Vanderheim suggested, "Your marital problems can wait for later, Grif. I'm paying you — and paying you well — for one thing. Her signature on a bill of sale. Now let's get on with it."

Gracie asked, "What does the Colonel have to say about this?" The question was a delaying tactic, more than anything else. She doubted very much that Colonel Vanderheim knew his wife had formed an alliance with Grif — or that pressure was being applied to a woman in a wheelchair.

"None of your bus—" began Grif.

But Mrs. Vanderheim drew herself to her full height and said, haughtily, "*I've* always made the important decisions. While *the Colonel* has the appearance, he lacks the will for business." She dismissed him with a wave of her hand. "He's weak. If I were to depend on him, we'd be paupers."

There's more than one kind of poverty, Gracie thought, and *the worst is when you have no wealth of soul.*

Three rapid knocks sounded on the door. Making a slicing motion across his neck, Grif moved purposely toward Gillian.

"You there, Gracie?"

Herb, of course. In shining armor.

A pause.

Lacey took a step toward the door — but Grif caught Gillian on either shoulder, from behind the wheelchair, and Lacey stopped short.

Eventually, Gracie heard Herb moving away.

"But he'll be back," Grif said in a low growl. "By then, these papers will be signed . . . or else."

Now what, Lord? There are three of us, but we're still outnumbered in muscle and mobility — though never, if You're on our side. Just give me an idea, Lord — something that will keep him from hurting Gillian — or any of us. Because I'm nearly certain, if he gets her signature, he won't leave us here to testify that she was threatened. She shivered. *What I wouldn't give for a sling, Lord, and a few smooth stones.*

"Give me your apron, Parks." To Mrs. Vanderheim, he said, "Use the strings to tie them up. The kid first."

Lord, surely he knows there's rope here. From where they stood, Gracie could see two large coils, looped around spikes. *Does he really expect two apron strings to hold us both?* Nevertheless, she removed the apron, ripped off the strings, and tossed them in Mrs. Vanderheim's direction.

Advancing to Mrs. Pomeroy, papers and pen extended, Grif sneered, "Well, aren't we being helpful?"

Not really, Gracie thought, an idea forming. She raised an eyebrow at Lacey, nodded toward the door, and Lacey moved quickly in that direction, forcing Mrs. Vanderheim to follow. Slowly, Gracie sidled to the crate of metal parts, loaded three without sharp edges into the body of her apron, and knotted the corners to form a bag. It wasn't heavy enough to do too much damage, she hoped — just enough.

Help my aim, Lord, she prayed, and called Grif's name.

He turned, scowling.

She swirled the packet around twice — then threw it with all her strength, aiming for his chest. It hit his stomach, instead, and with a gigantic OOF! he released the papers, doubled over and fell to his knees.

"Strings!" Gracie demanded, and while Mrs. Vanderheim stood with her mouth open, Lacey snatched the apron strings, ran over and tied Grif's feet together, ending with a small, neat double bow.

Gracie, grabbing a rope, took care of his hands while Lacey ran past Mrs. Vanderheim — still immobilized — and unlatched the door, throwing it open. "Hey! Hey!" she called. "We're in here! Help!"

As Herb replaced the rope with handcuffs and untied the bow from around Grif's ankles, Lacey told him excitedly, "Gracie took that bag of metal stuff and threw it Ka-WHOP! — just like with Goliath!"

"David and Goliath." Herb smiled and pulled a silent Grif to his feet.

"No! Goliath and *Gram!* Remember, Gracie? The rooster I told you about? And the snowball? You did to Uncle Grif what Gram did to *that* Goliath!"

Gillian Pomeroy rubbed her throat, then said haltingly, "Except . . . Sunday dinner. . . ."

Lacey giggled. "The snowball killed that old rooster," she explained. "Gram said he made the best chicken dinner she ever ate!"

13

It was wonderfully heartening to know that Grif was safely confined in one of Herb's cells.

It seemed that Kelly felt it, too. Her forehead was suddenly free of so many worry lines, as she sat at Gracie's kitchen table, a cup of tea steaming before her. "What will they charge him with?" she asked quietly.

"A whole laundry list, I'd think." Gracie wondered, though, if any of it would keep him in jail for long. She reached to cover Kelly's hand with her own.

Kelly cleared her throat. "Would it help if I testified?"

Gracie paused. "They can't force you to."

"But can they force me *not* to?"

Gracie closed her eyes. *Lord, I have no idea what this poor young woman has been through with that man, but I ask that You touch her spirit and her heart —*

"Are you *praying?*" Kelly now sounded so much like Lacey, that Gracie had to smile. "Yes. I'm praying for you, dear."

"Could you . . . do it out loud? Could we . . . pray together?"

Thank You, Lord!

"Of course we can!" They clasped hands and bowed their heads. So intent were they on their thoughts, they gasped in unison as the doorbell broke their spirit-filled mood.

Colonel Vanderheim stood beyond the screen door. For a moment, Gracie couldn't speak, couldn't even think. Then she remembered her manners. "Come in, Colonel," she said. "We're just having a cup of tea."

He seemed as well groomed as he had been when she first met him on Cordelia's porch, but some of his suavity had left him. When he saw Kelly, he rushed to her, catching both her hands in his. Falling to one knee was a bit theatrical, Gracie felt, but perhaps not where he came from.

"I can't begin to tell you, my dear, how pained I am that you and your mother have been put through such trials. And that my wife —" His voice cracked.

Is he sincere, Lord? She had felt, earlier, that he was. And she still wanted to believe so, especially when she saw the stricken look in his eyes as he rose unsteadily and said, "I wonder, Mrs. Parks. Perhaps, that tea?"

While more water heated, she opened a container of small sticky buns left over from the Family Day. He brightened considerably as she offered him one. Savoring the first bite, he said, "You can think you know someone so thoroughly —" His voice broke, but another taste seemed to restore his courage. "I knew that she was — ambitious. More than I. But I never thought —" Even the sticky bun lacked sufficient magic. He laid it on the table and bowed his head. "How can I make it up to Mrs. Pomeroy?"

"And what happens to your project, Colonel? Without her property?"

He shrugged. "Another site will be found. Somewhere." He managed a small smile. "Although not, I hope, within her protest-and-picket territory." His eyes sparkled, and he reached for the sticky bun again. "I'd already given up on the cemetery. That lady —" he nodded to Kelly — "your mother — is exceptional! You must be very proud of her."

"I am," Kelly said, in a tone that seemed at first surprised, then confident. "I am, indeed!"

Gracie had forgotten, with everything else that was going on, the threatening tone of that last note found at the church. So it

came as a surprise to her, as the choir pro-
cessed, to see the bouquet of moneyplant
and artificial red carnations on the altar, behind the cross. So someone had taken the
threat seriously, or else decided that it
would do no harm to give in to such a mild
threat. Perhaps someone had placed them
there without having any idea of their
meaning. In any event they *were* there now.
And the most important question was —
how would the swapper interpret that fact?

Compared with Grif and the other entan-
glements, however, the swaps seemed more
prankish than menacing.

God, Creator, loving Father . . .
We gather to worship Thee!
Jesus, Shepherd, Savior, Brother . . .
We assemble to worship Thee!
Holy Spirit, be a part of each troubled,
    yearning heart;
Be within us, here today
As we praise . . . as we pray —
Holy Spirit, Christ our Savior,
    God our Father —
One from Three!
We come gladly to worship Thee!
A . . . men.

As the choir proclaimed its welcome to

the congregation of worshipers, suddenly there came a disturbance from the back of the sanctuary.

Gracie stiffened. Pastor Paul, sitting in one of the large chairs, rose now to peer out from the pulpit in an attempt to determine what was happening.

With the ceremony usually reserved for coronations, the head usher now advanced to the front of the church and handed a note to him, explaining that it had been placed where a candle-stand normally sat.

Paul opened it, glanced at Gracie, and asked a question with his eyebrows.

She nodded.

He scanned the congregation and began reading:

"LET THERE BE LIGHT," SAID OUR CREATOR GOD,
AND SET HIS LIGHTS IN SKIES OF NIGHT AND DAY.
AND THEN HE SENT HIS LIGHT INTO THE WORLD
TO TEACH AND PREACH AND SHOW US ALL THE WAY.

NOW, IN HIS CHURCHES, LIGHT PORTRAYS HIS LOVE:
LIGHT THROUGH THE STAINED-

GLASS WINDOWS, SUNNY
    DAYS;
LIGHT FROM THE CHANDELIERS,
    SO FAR ABOVE;
AND THEN THOSE OTHER
    LIGHTS THAT FLICKER, FLAME,
AND LIFT THEIR GLOW TO
    GLORIFY HIS NAME.

YET WHEN A SERVANT OF THE
    LORD GOES EMPTY-HANDED
    TO HIS TASK —

WHAT HAPPENS, THEN, TO
    CANDLELIGHT? WE ASK.

Gracie knew that a ransom "demand"
would follow, but Pastor Paul refolded the
paper, placed it in his pocket, and offered an
altered Call to Worship.

"We come into the house and presence of
the God of all light," he said earnestly,
"asking that He illuminate any darkened
corners of our lives . . . that He so ignite our
hearts and minds and spirits that we reflect
His Light and Love in every thought, word
and action."

How far this young man has come, Gracie
told the Lord. *How he has grown in knowledge
and love and confidence.*

★ ★ ★

Even with the disturbance, it was a lovely service. The brass music stand gleamed and the bouquet — artificial carnations notwithstanding — looked beautiful behind the cross. *Whoever this "thief" is, Lord,* she commented as the choir stood for the anthem, *he's contributing a great deal to the beauty of our church.* She missed the first phrase as the thought struck her. Beauty! That sort of sensitivity to the aesthetics of whatever was going on made Gracie realize, suddenly, that maybe the culprit was female.

Why hadn't she thought of that before? Surely, if her head hadn't been going in so many directions, she would have. Actually, lollipops and Beatrix Potter and solid brass music stands seemed more like choices being made by a woman's sensibility.

Determined to pay attention, she nonetheless soon found her thoughts wandering over the congregation. Kelly was there — and had beamed with pride during the anthem as Lacey sang in the front row. When the choir left the loft, Lacey had rushed to join her aunt and now nestled against her. Gracie thanked God for both of them.

Still, who could the trickster be, she wondered. Was he — *or she* — in attendance this morning? Why hadn't she thought to scan the congregation while Pastor Paul read the latest note? Would some change of expression have given away the "perp," as Herb might call him? *Or her,* she hastened to add.

"Let us pray," Pastor Paul said.

Oh, Lord, Gracie thought, chagrined. *I've frittered away this whole service, I might as well have been sleeping . . . even at home in bed. I do so ask Your forgiveness.*

Her distress must have remained on her face. As soon as she saw him, Uncle Miltie mock-scowled back at her. "Gracie," he said, his tone a mixture of concern and authority, "this afternoon, you're taking a good, long nap!"

Impulsively, she hugged him. "I might just do that!"

But first, there was Paul, waiting for her. "No ransom demand this time?" she asked him.

"Oh, yes!" He fished for the note and slipped it to her. "But I haven't opened it yet." They walked toward his office.

"Mm-hmmm." She opened the note and stopped so suddenly she threw him off balance. "Now — what do you suppose *this* means!"

Chuckling, he said, "I have no idea — until you show me what *this* is."

She indicated the last line of the printed message.

RANSOM: NEXT SUNDAY, CELEBRATE CHRISTMAS!

"An exciting idea." Abe Wasserman placed a pitcher of iced tea in the center of the table. "May I join you?"

Rocky, who had sat down with Gracie at the deli, chuckled. "Would it be Sunday if we three friends failed to share a meal?"

Abe pulled out a chair. "You bring such interesting dilemmas. For these, I credit you, Gracie Lynn Parks. Where you go, intrigue follows."

"Often," she said, "it gets there before I do."

He tapped the note. "But this one! To celebrate a winter holy day in the warmest season of the year — this requires imagination. And yet — wisdom."

Gracie and Rocky waited, sipping tea.

"Should not all the holidays be so extended? Perhaps not their trappings, but their basic principles. The reason for their being. Should not each day be Passover, for example — remembering God's miraculous saving of His people from slavery? And Yom Kippur . . . should we not *always* confess our guilts and plead forgiveness?"

Amy Cantrell, trim in a summery skirt and plain white apron, was listening in. "There's a big department store in Mason City that always has 'Christmas in July' sales." She smiled sunnily. "And what Eternal Hope has to offer's a lot better than jeans at half-price!"

Abe said fondly, "For a teenager, I'd think little could top such a bargain!"

She confided, "I bought three pairs last time. It took most of my tip money, even then. Which reminds me." She fished her pad from her pocket. "What can I get you today?"

She was still jotting down their orders when the door swished open and Pastor Paul called, "Is there room for one more?"

Only Rocky failed to give a hearty welcome. Gracie glanced to see just how stormy his expression would be. With these two friends, the weather could be unpredictable. But Rocky's face read only "partly cloudy."

Relieved, she moved her chair a little to make room for the sandy-haired young minister. Without preamble, he indicated the note. "What's your take on this?"

They reviewed what had already been said.

He nodded. "Ideas have been swirling in my head ever since church — what we could do with this. Gracie, could you take notes? You know my handwriting."

Rocky said, "Let me." His ever-present pad appeared, and he poised his ballpoint pen. "Fire away."

" 'Joy to the World,' " Pastor Paul began. "That joy should be an everyday thing." He nodded to Abe, "Just as you were saying. There are dozens of other hymns with the theme of joy . . . without the Christmas tag."

" 'Joyful, Joyful, We Adore Thee,' " Gracie contributed.

"Exactly!"

"Do you want me to write all this down?" Rocky asked.

"As much as you can get." Pastor Paul grinned. "You newspaper people are good at that."

"Right," Rocky growled. "What's next?"

"If I may?" Abe's hands folded, index fingertips touching his lower lip.

"Please!" It seemed unanimous.

"Joy is not an exclusive property of Christmas — nor even of Christianity." He added softly, "This comes as no surprise?"

Pastor Paul nodded. " 'Joy cometh in the morning.' "

"And so many events — as what we celebrate in Purim."

"When Haman didn't get to wipe out the

Jews." Amy plunked two baskets of warm onion rolls on the table.

"Ethnic cleansing, even then." Rocky shook his head.

"But we do not mention — that evil name." Abe's eyes twinkled.

Gracie frowned. "Haman?"

"No, no!" he chided. "Instead, we concentrate on the goodness, beauty and wisdom of Queen Esther!"

They waited quietly as Amy distributed salads. She said, "It'll be really neat, if we do Christmas. Maybe we could sing 'O, Holy Night.' Do you think so, Gracie?"

Rocky kept the pad and pen handy as they ate and talked.

By the time dessert was served — date and pear strudel with cream — Rocky had filled a third page of notes, and everyone seemed equally excited about the next week's service.

"So you have determined," Abe said, "there is no danger in bowing to the demands of this swap-minded thief?"

Amy took the iced-tea pitcher and replaced it with a full one. "But everything's always returned. And the music stand. . . ." Her voice trailed off. "We never did give the kids their lollipops. And nothing bad has happened."

"So far," Rocky added.

They finished their strudel in silence.

Uncle Miltie was asleep when Gracie arrived home and therefore unable to enforce his order that she take a nap. His niece was perhaps as disappointed as relieved. She might feel better for a little extra rest, but she hated to waste time, especially on such a lovely afternoon.

Gooseberry lay curled beside Uncle Miltie on the couch, but no sooner had Gracie eased the screen door shut than he landed with a soft plop on the braided throw-rug and came running to purr around her ankles.

"No, Gooseberry," she whispered, "no long walk today, I'm afraid. But how would you feel about a short one — to Cordelia's, to see Lacey and her aunt?"

His quick appearance at the screen door — his luxurious tail at full attention — seemed to indicate approval.

"Just a minute, then. I'll leave a note for Uncle Miltie."

They found Lacey in her favorite spot — draped over the tire swing. A banana popsicle dripped from her hand, and even when she saw them, she smiled only slightly. "It's a bad day," she confided, before Gracie could ask. "I have to leave soon."

Gracie felt a catch in her heart. She had realized from the beginning that this child would be special to her, but had also understood from the start that her stay in Willow Bend was temporary, dependent on her aunt's decisions, her grandmother's condition and the ultimate opening of school. But she found herself unprepared for the wrenching thought of losing her so soon.

Masking her feelings, she observed, "Mason City isn't far away."

"But, Gracie, I can't drive!"

"I can. Kelly can."

"But *will* you? Will *she?* She'll have Gram to take care of — at least for a while — and even when Gram's better, it will be a long time 'til *she* can drive again. After Aunt Kelly's gone back to the city and her job — though," she added, looking brighter by several watts, "she may not. Go back, I mean. At least never to that awful Grif."

Well, Gracie thought, if justice serves, he won't be available for going back to, anyway, not for a long while.

Lacey swung back and forth. Gooseberry watched the movement of her feet, the end of his tail flicking. "I'll miss choir. And helping you, Gracie! Who'll chop nuts for you?"

"Well, you're not gone yet!" Gracie said,

"and for Rocky's lunch I'll need someone to do just that! Do you think you'll be free?"

"Oh, yes!" She righted herself, dropping her popsicle in the process. "You can have it, Gooseberry," she said magnanimously. "Wait 'til I go ask Aunt Kelly!"

Cordelia called from the porch swing, "Come sit a spell, Gracie!"

Gracie started. "I hadn't even noticed you."

"A good innkeeper learns to blend in. We hear more that way."

Gracie settled into one of the wrought-iron chairs, not yet returned to the lawn. "Is Colonel Vanderheim still here?"

"He left this morning, just after breakfast."

Gracie nodded, encouraging her to continue.

"I suppose you heard he's resigning from his company."

Gracie couldn't help herself. "Really!"

Cordelia sniffed. "I figured you'd know that, too, since you seem to know everything else." She stood abruptly, the swing swerving and banging behind her. "Well, I have things to do. I guess you do, too, with another catering job this week. Isn't it about time you slow down — let some of the younger folks take over?"

The door swished behind her, and Gracie came so close to sputtering she could feel the ends of her hair spark. That Cordelia! She was only two months younger than Gracie.

Lord, it's a bit disturbing that everyone keeps telling me I should slow down. And while I appreciate that — well, I don't like hearing it. What do You say, Lord? All of these opportunities bring me closer to people — and to You. It seems You want me to be involved . . . or is it just that I want to? Could You let me know, it doesn't matter how —

"Gracie!"

It was Cordelia, halfway in and halfway out of her front door. "You'd best get on home. Uncle Miltie called, and he sounds real upset!"

14

Gracie was breathless when she turned in from the street, past a small silver car she knew she should recognize. Uncle Miltie — looking rumpled and a bit frantic, but all in one piece, thank goodness — met her on the porch.

"That woman's here!" he sighed, "and I don't know what to do with her!"

Gracie was about to ask what woman, but it became all too apparent.

"Eudora!" she said, shooing Uncle Miltie in the direction of his hammock and telling Gooseberry to keep him company, "how nice of you to visit!"

Eudora McAdoo looked after Uncle Miltie with what seemed like disappointment, but she followed Gracie through the kitchen into the dining room. "What lovely snapdragons!" She pinched one of the velvety red blossoms at the jaw to make it open. "Couldn't we just sit in the kitchen? Or better yet —" She looked toward the door through which Uncle Miltie had made his escape.

"The kitchen's fine!" Gracie retraced her steps, waved her unexpected guest to a stool, and went to the cupboard. "Would you like a cup of tea?"

"Please." Eudora settled atop the stool like a bluebird nesting. "With lemon."

Ah, yes, Gracie noticed, she was wearing blue, the tint of her morning's hair misted with a bluish cast.

"We have so much in common, dear." Mrs. McAdoo looked about the spacious kitchen. "I was never such a marvelous cook, I'll admit, but when we were home from our adventures, I did keep Mr. McAdoo well-fed — perhaps even contributing to his fatal heart attack, poor man. He did so love rich foods!" She sighed dramatically. "He was never much for vegetables — said that green was a color for money, not food — but we did keep a small flower garden, and snapdragons were always his favorite. Perhaps they're a flower that appeals particularly to men."

Gracie didn't rise to the bait. "Cream or sugar?"

"Just sugar, two lumps. Does George like snapdragons?"

Now, how should she answer that? "He and his wife," she said, suddenly inspired, "always found a place in their large garden for flowers. And yes, I believe there were sometimes snapdragons, though hollyhocks seemed to be a favorite."

Gracie set out a plate of tea cookies.

"Oh, I shouldn't —" but Eudora's hand hovered indecisively. "But they're from yesterday's gala, aren't they? And they'll spoil, if we don't." She selected two. "I do love tea. I remember having some exotic blend in small lacquered cups in a Japanese garden, where paper lanterns swung in a slight breeze, and a young man with marvelous cheekbones and hair like jet beading cooked over a flaming brazier. . . ."

Two cups, six cookies and five exotic anecdotes later, Eudora McAdoo slid from the stool and said, "I really must go. They'll be gathering for the dinner hour, and I do enjoy chatting with my friends. But first I must say good-bye to dear George."

Whether Uncle Miltie had foreseen her departure, or had simply decided to take a walk with Gooseberry, the hammock was empty.

Was it Gracie's imagination, however, or was it still swinging, as though its occupant had made a hasty escape?

"Oh, dear. Well, do tell him how I enjoyed seeing him again, won't you?" And Eudora was off.

Gracie stayed to enjoy the air, beginning to cool a little, then went inside to scrub vegetables for a relish tray. She was glad that Uncle Miltie didn't agree with Mr. McAdoo's assessment of green foods.

The table was set, a ham-and-noodle casserole reheating in the microwave, and everything else ready, when Uncle Miltie peered from the doorway to the living room and asked in a stage whisper, "Is it safe?"

She asked mischievously, "Is it my cooking that's so frightening?"

He refused to play along. "She's gone?"

"Long ago. The meal's nearly ready."

"Danger stimulates my appetite." He inhaled deeply and licked his lips. "I'll wash up."

When he returned, he apologized for not having set the table, at least.

She didn't ask him — until he'd pushed back sufficiently to allow room for strawberry shortcake — "Are you really afraid of her, Uncle Miltie?"

He took a long time to answer — longer than his attention even to shortcake usually required. When he did speak, it was in a slow, thoughtful tone. "I'm not sure 'afraid' is the word. But when Dora and I were courting, I made all the moves. You know what I mean? It scares me that these young women are so . . . *aggressive!*"

She nearly choked on whipped topping. "How old do you think Eudora is?"

He shrugged. "Older than you. Younger than me. Besides," he said, patting his rounded stomach, "I have no intention of leaving you, Gracie — that is, not until you kick me out." He scratched his chin. "I have nothing against being friends with women — and she's interesting to listen to. It's just that *look* in her eye, and it's there most of the time. Unfortunately."

Even though Marge was unable to help at the event itself on Wednesday, Gracie contemplated her next catering task without too much concern. It should be a breeze, after the last two. There would be only fifteen guests, Rocky had assured her at first, just people associated with the paper, to honor those who'd won awards in a recent Midwestern competition. "Just give us cold cuts, cheeses, relish plate, some salads — potato, macaroni, chicken, pasta, fresh fruit, Jello — and a couple of your fabulous desserts. Oh," he added as an afterthought, "I did say they should invite families. Maybe some friends. Better plan for fifty or seventy or so, just in case. But don't make a big deal out of it. Whatever you do, I know it'll be great! And I did promise your special sandwich rolls."

She had waited, in case there were more addendums, but he seemed to be finished — and apparently convinced that what he was asking was a small thing, indeed. She wondered how he'd react if she asked for a special edition of the *Mason County Gazette* — nothing big, just an eight-page spread, or maybe twenty-four, with color photos.

Still, on Tuesday, while Lacey chopped nuts and Uncle Miltie scrubbed potatoes, Gracie was able to work and think . . . even to discuss some important items with the Lord.

Are we right to plan a "Christmas" celebration for Sunday? Everyone so far was excited about it, but would it send a wrong message to the trickster — inviting more serious events? Still, could it ever be wrong to recognize the wonder of Your coming to earth?

"You're awfully quiet, Gracie." Lacey hadn't been able to quell the stars in her eyes all morning, knowing her grandmother would be reunited with her the next day.

"I guess I was thinking."

"We could sing while we work."

"What would you like to sing?"

" 'What Child Is This?' "

Gracie smiled. She loved that song! Actually, she loved nearly all Christmas music.

15

The next morning, with everything in readiness for Rocky's luncheon, Gracie walked to Cordelia Fountain's. Kelly and Lacey would be leaving that day, taking Gillian Pomeroy back to her home in Mason City for further recuperation.

Cordelia had set a formal tea for the occasion — never matter that Lacey's cup held lemonade and Gillian's only ice water. "Do join us, Gracie," Cordelia called. "If I'd known you were coming, I'd have begged some of your tea cakes. I fear mine will be like bullets!" Hands clasped before her, she eyed each bite as it was taken, and relaxed into light laughter only when everyone assured her that they were wonderful.

"I'm sure they don't come close to my dear mother's. Hers were divine, but I never inherited the knack."

"They're very good," Kelly assured her, putting one on a plate for her mother who was seated beside her in her wheelchair.

"Yummy." Lacey took another.

Gracie said, "You have nothing to apologize for, Cordelia. They're moist and flavorful."

Lacey was at Gracie's elbow. "Doesn't Gram look wonderful?"

She did indeed. Gracie said, "Mrs. Pomeroy, I know you can't remember me —"

"Oh, but I do." The woman's voice was rich and warm, her smile bright, and the slim hand she extended trembling only a little.

Gracie accepted it into hers.

"I guess," Mrs. Pomeroy said, "I gave everyone a fright. But —" she laughed lightly, "fortunately, I slept through most of it."

Kelly moved behind her mother, bending to kiss her cheek. "So nice to have you back, Mom. I never knew how much I loved you until —" She groped for a tissue, then dabbed at her eyes with the collar of her shirt.

"Well, I'm fine now!" Gillian thumped the arm of her wheelchair. "And don't think you'll keep me in this thing much longer!"

"Ready to take to the barricades again?" Kelly teased.

"Actually, yes!"

"Gram!" Lacey stiffened, her eyes wide.

Gillian Pomeroy reached to draw her close. "My dear, there's so much wrong in

269

this wonderful world. How can I rest unless I do my part to right it?"

"But can't the world get along without you until you're better?"

Gillian's eyes grew dreamy. "Did you happen to see TV last night, any of you? The special about how animals are abused? I already have some costumes — actually enough for all three of us, if you'd push my wheelchair, Kelly."

"Mom!"

"Gram!"

Gracie would have loved to stay for the rest of the discussion — although she had no doubt who would win — but it was time to collect Uncle Miltie and Marge, and be about her catering business. "I hate to say good-bye, but I must. Lacey, Kelly, Mrs. Pomeroy, please drop by any time. It's been wonderful getting to know you." She opened her arms, and Lacey rushed into them.

"I'll miss you so much, Gracie!"

"And I'll miss you." She released the child with a final pat and a kiss on the top of her head. "Lovely tea, Cordelia. Thank you so much for including me."

They all beamed at one another.

At the newspaper office, Rocky helped unload the food. "We'll go in here, Gracie. We've set up more tables."

Fortunately, Gracie had brought enough long white table cloths so that the scars from markers and pens and — apparently — knives wouldn't be seen. Uncle Miltie and Barb covered each long table, while Gracie followed with a narrow edging that carried the word *Congratulations* in many colors.

"Thought I told you not to go to a lot of trouble," Rocky said, his arms full of trophies. "Where do I put these?"

Gracie indicated what would be the buffet table. She'd brought a floor-length skirt for it. Uncle Miltie had divided his snapdragons — those that were still fresh enough — into slender milkglass vases for each of several tables, and Barb had shaped five larger centerpieces with roses, glads, white hosta, dusty miller and a variety of vining sprays.

"Will there be any room for the food?" Rocky teased, and Uncle Miltie paused, his face a study in dismay.

"Oh," he said, "you expected food, too?"

"Rascal!" Gracie accused, but laughed with the others.

By the time bowls and platters were arranged, thirty-five people had assembled. Barb at that point left to meet a piano student, while Gracie already began planning what she might do with all the leftovers.

Uncle Miltie whispered, "You mind if I go? Gooseberry and I could spend the afternoon in the hammock. I could come back later. If you need me?"

She waved him on. "Rocky will help load. Are you sure you want to walk that far?"

"Be good for me." Giving a little wave, he moved as quietly as his walker would allow him. As he struggled with the outside door, Gracie rose from her chair, but Rocky was already there, helping him out with a pat to the shoulder and a thank-you.

Dear Rocky. What a nice man he was!

It was heartening to Gracie that their small paper had been singled out for several awards. She had seen the announcement in the paper, of course, but it seemed so much more real here, with the pleased recipients and their proud families eating lunch.

Suddenly a messenger arrived, handed a small envelope to Rocky and left, eyeing the buffet table.

"Gracie?" Rocky called out. She started. What was this? Had he planned something to embarrass her? He waved the envelope.

Curious, she went forward to claim it. Rocky winked at her. Did he know what was in it? Or not?

Back in her seat, she turned the envelope

in her hands. Her name was printed in the block letters with which she had become so familiar.

But why was it addressed only to her? And why, unlike the others, had it not been left at the church?

She opened it and read:

THIS IS MY FINAL OFFER.
YOU'RE WEARY; SO AM I,
BUT THIS NEW "THING" I'M
   TAKING,
I'D PLANNED TO, BY AND BY.

SURROUNDS "ITSELF" WITH
   METAL,
BUT NOT OF METAL MADE —
PERHAPS AT ONE TIME CROWNED
   WITH BROWN,
BUT NOW SUPREMELY GRAYED . . .
TALLER THAN MUSIC STAND OF
   BRASS —
STILL, MUSIC IS "ITS" HEART,
MORE FLEXIBLE THAN WOODEN,
WITH LAUGHTER AS "ITS" ART.

RANSOM: A PICNIC LUNCH FOR
   TWO DELIVERED BY GRACIE
   LYNN PARKS. 2:30 P.M. TODAY,
   AT MARSH'S MEADOW.

There was no question, she knew, scanning it a second time for its rather clever clues; Uncle Miltie had been kidnapped. And she was fairly certain she knew by whom.

"So, what was it?" Rocky asked.

Gracie realized that while she had sat there, caught in thought, the group was dispersing.

"The note," Rocky prompted.

She handed it to him.

Several of the staff and guests detoured to where Gracie sat.

"Great spread, Gracie!"

"I may just divorce my wife. Are you available?"

"Best eats this side of Mason City. Maybe even the Mississippi!"

"Thanks a bunch!"

She responded to each, as Rocky studied the note again.

He frowned. "It sounds like —"

"It is," she said, and added calmly, "Uncle Miltie's been kidnapped."

"You don't sound as upset as I would have expected."

"The ransom sounds innocent enough. And easy to provide."

He glanced at the buffet table. "You think he knew?"

"Yes, I think 'he' did."

Rocky consulted his watch. "We have half an hour. Let's get cracking."

Marsh's Meadow lay several miles out of town. Throughout the year, sheep wandered the grassier areas. A pattern of fences and gates allowed access to other spaces when the forage needed a chance to replenish itself.

A small silver car stood near an open gate, beyond which a gravel path — grooved deeply with heavy tracks — led to a wooded area.

"I see them," Rocky said, and added semi-lightly, "He doesn't seem to be gagged and bound."

"Escape might be impossible, via walker," Gracie replied.

"You don't think he's . . . frightened."

She laughed. "Maybe *she* should be!"

But Uncle Miltie's mood, when they eased to a stop, could have been described as almost mellow. Even before the van's engine died, he called to Gracie, "She's moving to Georgia! To live with her daughter."

And she understood that his cheerful mood spelled relief.

He fought his walker over the pocked terrain. "You weren't scared, Gracie, were you?"

"Only for a moment," she assured him.

Eudora said comfortably, "I knew you'd figure it out. Actually this was the whole point of my campaign, right from the first — a romantic picnic with George, here."

Suddenly, Gracie noticed, her uncle was beginning to show a bit of discomfort. She decided to rescue him. "Miltie dear, will you help Rocky unload the van? Eudora and I will use these cloths to cover a spot. Let's get this picnic on the road!"

During the preparations, Gooseberry appeared, apparently having concluded a successful reconnoiter.

"You kidnapped Gooseberry, too!"

Eudora giggled. "I had no choice. It was both, or neither." She hugged a bowl of potato salad to her and said more soberly, "I admired George from the very first I saw him — I suppose you knew that. What a wonderful wit! And it seemed — well, how better to attract a trickster than to become a trickster oneself!"

Gracie said drily, "You did it quite well."

"Thanks. Actually, it became quite a challenge. And a great deal of fun. I came close to getting caught several times — and I was just a teensy bit concerned that people might be alarmed."

Fortunately, she didn't ask if they had been.

She set down the bowl. Sunlight touched her lavender hair, a perfect match for the violets imprinted on her shirt and down the outside seams of her slacks.

She's really quite pretty, Gracie thought, and wondered why Uncle Miltie hadn't been smitten, even without trickery — or snapdragons.

"I guess," Eudora sighed, unloading silverware from a plastic tub, "George is one of those men for whom one woman is enough for a lifetime."

Gracie said gently, "They were very much in love."

"And he's content living with you."

"I hope so."

"And Gooseberry, of course."

Hearing his name, a certain cat sauntered over and loftily accepted tribute.

"And you — ?" Gracie asked, a catch in her throat.

"One day at a time." She smiled. "Dear Gracie, I wasn't consumed by passion, or anything. In fact," she said contemplatively, "I'm quite satisfied with the way everything turned out! It's been great fun, watching people guess . . . and, I'll admit, discomfiting a certain someone in the soprano section — more than a little!"

Despite herself, Gracie laughed.

"And I've gotten to know you dear people. My life is much, much richer for this short time in Willow Bend. When I'm old, I'll remember these times with pleasure. Meanwhile, I hope you'll allow me still to look forward to my Christmas out of season on Sunday."

She winked.

They all laughed.

Soon they settled down to eat, and as Eudora began regaling Uncle Miltie with one of her monologues, Rocky seized the moment to whisper to Gracie, "Did she say *when* she's old?"

Gracie nodded. "But I don't think she ever will be."

He chewed on a chicken wing. "Neither will you, Gracie. Isn't it amazing how much better food tastes out of doors?"

What amazed Gracie was that he could eat so heartily so soon again.

But what she said was, "Everything about life is amazing!" *Thank You, Lord!*

Gooseberry, nibbling on an edge of pastry, meowed emphatic agreement.

Recipe

Gracie's Chicken-and-Onion Bake

2 large red onions, sliced
8 chicken thighs with skin on
Dijon mustard
Thyme
Rosemary
Freshly ground pepper
¼ cup olive oil

Preheat oven to 300 degrees F. Cover the bottom of a baking dish with a thick layer of the onion slices. Lay the chicken pieces on top, skin side up. Slather the mustard generously over the chicken. Lightly crush together one teaspoon each of thyme and rosemary and then sprinkle across top, along with freshly ground pepper to taste. Gently drizzle the olive oil over everything. Bake 1½ hours, or until chicken pieces are deep golden-brown on top.

Don't oil the dish or use too much oil on top. The chicken makes most of the moisture, with the low, slow cooking. And the mustard is sufficiently salty so that no extra salt is needed. Eventually the onions will turn soft and sweet, their texture almost like a sauce.

In order to vary the dish, you can include some sliced potatoes with the onion, and perhaps a sprinkling of crumbled bacon around the chicken. If you want a bit of color, a little chopped parsley on top looks pretty, of course. (My method for chopping parsley: I put a sprig or two in a juice glass and cut it, using scissors inside the glass. You have small pieces in an instant, ready to shake out over the dish.)

This serves four but also makes delicious leftovers. You'll want crusty bread to soak up the onion sauce and chicken juices.

About the Author

"Where I go, clutter happens," admits Evelyn Minshull, author of twenty-plus published books, erstwhile artist, compulsive teacher, gardener, baker-of-cookies and knitter-of-booties she gives away — often to strangers. Every Sunday, spring through fall, she takes flowers to church. It's a habit begun long ago and now continued in her mother's memory.

"Mother taught a reverence for words. My father encouraged my art. But Freddie and our three daughters not only survived my clutter, they participated in a multitude of crafts and puppet performances that grew from it. And the girls were my best literary critics — ever."

Valerie, Melanie, and Robin are grown and gone now, living in Kentucky, North Carolina and central Pennsylvania. Granddaughter Micky attends Vanderbilt University. Grandsons Jonathan and Benjamin are in elementary school. But Fred, husband and unflagging encourager, still steps casually around piles of books.

Fred built their ranch-style home on three acres of former apple orchard and sheep pasture. Pennsylvania white-tailed deer, enticed by fallen apples, trespass from their refuge in the lower half-acre (once a pasture for the daughters' horses and now a tangle of shrubs and lofty oaks).

"This is my favorite place on earth," Evelyn says.

Fred only smiles.

The employees of Walker Large Print hope you have enjoyed this Large Print book. All our Large Print titles are designed for easy reading, and all our books are made to last. Other Walker Large Print books are available at your library, through selected bookstores, or directly from us.

For information about titles, please call:
  (800) 223-1244

To share your comments, please write:
  Publisher
  Walker Large Print
  295 Kennedy Memorial Drive
  Waterville, ME   04901

Guideposts magazine and the Daily Guideposts annual devotion book are available in large-print format by contacting:
  Guideposts Customer Service
  39 Seminary Hill Road
  Carmel, NY 10512
or
  www. guideposts.com